MURDER DOUBLE DIPPED

Books by Gary Doc Nelson

A MORAL STANCE: The fictionalized true story of the 1951 University of San Francisco football team and their stand against discrimination.

THE VIKING SAGA SERIES

HAMER
FALCONI'S GIFT
HAWK'S BREW
THE BLACK SPOT
GUN'S SONG
THE VOYAGE HOME (TO BE RELEASED IN 2025)

THE ROB MACKAY SPEED-DATING MURDER SERIES

THE SPEED-DATING MURDERS
A RITUAL DEATH
THE PERFECT MURDER
THE CASE OF THE DETECTIVE DOG

MURDER DOUBLE DIPPED
DEATH BY CHOCOLATE To be published in 2025

All covers for the Rob MacKay - Speed-Dating Murder Series developed by Brian Van Cameric

MURDER DOUBLE DIPPED

GARY DOC NELSON

Waterside Productions

First Printing, 2025

ISBN-13: 978-1-968401-00-9 print edition
ISBN-13: 978-1-968401-01-6 e-book edition

Waterside Productions
2055 Oxford Ave
Cardiff, CA 92007
www.waterside.com

CHAPTER 1

Getting by security in the 560 Mission building was the hard part. Not the normal security features that one might think of–the cameras, the guard in the locked lobby, the needed credentials–but the security that was built into the building itself. There were elevators that only serviced certain floors. Stairwells that only connected two floors, and then only if the same firm occupied both floors. There was a fire escape stairwell that opened to all floors, but once in, you couldn't exit any floor except the lobby entrance.

He entered the building, flashing the necessary credentials, and took the elevator up to his floor. His was one of the five offices off the lobby into which the bank of elevators emptied. The office was one of the efficiency units in the building. It consisted of a reception area, a bathroom, and a small main office. He took off his suit, putting on khaki pants, black Nike shoes, and a black ski mask with a distinctive red stripe across the mouth. He picked up his weapon, an Uzi that he had sent to his office in parts, some packed with an Italian cappuccino maker. He walked quickly across the lobby to the door leading to the fire stairwell. He opened it, entered, and held it open a crack with a piece of wood, wedged between it and the floor. There would be no lock tampering on this door. If it closed, he wouldn't be able to get back in. He climbed in the dark to floor 31. He made sure his flesh-colored latex gloves were pulled tight to his wrists, covering the cuffs of his white shirt. He took a deep breath and unlocked the door, using the electronic key that defeated the door's security measure. He checked the safety on the Uzi, clicking it forward. It had been expensive assembling the weapon from parts, but it meant there was no serial number and no paper trail, a ghost gun with no past. He checked the magazine: twelve shots of Black Talon hollow point bullets in the twenty-five-shot magazine, a number crucial to his plan. He opened the door fully and stepped into the lobby of the law firm.

His target was exactly 130 feet away in a corner office, the space between them filled with desks, partitions, and people. It was quickly cleared of the latter when he ran through the room, firing three shots in the air. A woman–he couldn't tell if she was foolish, brave, or frozen in panic–stood in front of the corner office door. He shot her in the leg. Four shots used. The door had a sign that said *Lester Fisher, Managing Partner.* He kicked it open. His target stood beside his desk, his hands high above his head. The gunman shot three times. The bullets passed through the target's body, one of them shattering the window at his back.

The murderer turned and ran past the screaming woman, who was holding her leg with both hands, the blood staining the carpet beneath her. All the other occupants of the office had disappeared, hiding beneath their desks. He hadn't heard the elevator ding.

"If anyone sounds the alarm or tries to leave or use the elevator, I will kill them," he yelled.

There was no resistance. He ran to the stairwell, firing two more shots into the ceiling, and down three flights of stairs to the 28th floor. Again he unlocked the rigged door and ran into a lobby that had four doors to different businesses. He chose 2803. There were only two people there, a woman and a man. He'd only expected the man. He hesitated a few seconds looking at the woman, then moved the gun from the man and fired two shots at the woman–one to her head, one to her heart. Either would have killed her instantly. He pointed the gun at the man, who held up his hands. He swung the rifle at the man, missing his head, a move that allowed the man to grab him. They wrestled briefly, both trying to gain control of the gun. The murderer pulled the trigger and fired his last shot into the woman on the floor, then pushed the man, causing him to fall, still grasping the gun.

The murderer turned and ran. He heard the man behind him click on the empty rifle as he closed the door to the lobby and dropped a mask. He opened the fire door and ran back down the darkened stairwell to the office that held his clothes.

He picked up the wedge that had held his door open and went inside. The fire alarm sounded as he took off his clothes and shoes, putting them in a FedEx container and placing it with six other identical packages to be mailed the next day. He went to the bathroom, naked, and washed his face, hair, and hands thoroughly, then put on a new shirt and his suit. He slid his feet into expensive Italian loafers, combed his hair, and took a quick glance at himself in the mirror. He was done.

He looked at his watch. It had taken exactly two minutes and twenty-eight seconds, fifteen seconds less than he'd planned. He waited less than a minute before the fire alarm was shut off. The elevators now enabled, he took one to the third floor, where a cafeteria served breakfast and lunch for those who worked in the building. He grabbed bacon, eggs over easy, and coffee from the buffet, then waited for the inevitable shit storm. He hadn't planned the shooting of either woman, but the last one had been a plus.

The killer smiled to himself. It had taken four months to work out the plan. He'd practiced parts of it: bringing in and assembling the weapon, moving between floors, making sure his target was where he could find him. It was a plan worthy of a *Mission Impossible* script, without the gymnastics and exotic props. Broken down into parts, his plan was as simple as it was elegant. He'd heard that vengeance is a dish best served cold. The man felt like this was a banquet.

He brought his breakfast to an unoccupied table and thought back over what he had done, trying to find any error or deviation from the plan. Other than shooting the second woman, he could find none. He smiled. It had gone perfectly. That morning he had moved through ground-level security, as he did every day, wearing a suit and tie, the cards needed for access in his pocket. He'd taken the elevator to his office, well below the law offices of Braddock, Fisher, and Bunting. It had taken him a week to install the devices on the fire escape door locks on floor 28, as well as the one opening to 31 that would disable them at the push of a button. He'd checked the locator showing where the cell phone of his target was. He knew the office where he changed would be empty, the staff working remotely this Monday, a leftover from the COVID years.

He had just started eating when the police began arriving, their sirens blaring. He looked at his watch. It had been exactly four minutes and ten seconds since he'd fired his last shot. Others in the restaurant looked confused, then worried. Some of them stood. He did as well, looking around as if to ask, "What's happening?" No one entered the restaurant, but with sirens still arriving, an announcement boomed over the speakers that moments before had been playing soft music.

"There's been an incident involving gunfire in the building. Please stay where you are until further notice."

There were about 20 people in the café. All of them started talking at once. This was something he hadn't thought out—what to say when word of the shooting got out. Now he had at least an idea of how to react to the news.

"Did you hear anything?" he asked a woman standing at the next table.

"No," she said. "It must be on one of the upper floors."

"What if they come down here?" asked another woman, who had spilled her food across the table and was clutching her purse across her chest like a shield.

"The elevators don't work!" shouted a man by the bank of sliding doors as the fire alarm blared again.

Panic was beginning to grip many in the room.

"Please be seated," came the voice over the speaker system. "The police are in the building. They've shut down the elevators. They ask that you remain seated. The incident was many floors away. You are in no danger here. You will be free to go as soon as they secure the building."

The food in front of him was inviting; the murderer was hungry. He wanted to finish his bacon and eggs and perhaps even order a second dish, but he noticed that while many had taken their seats, none were eating. He took one bite and pushed his bowl away as if it tasted foul. He got up and moved to the table of the woman who was starting to panic.

"I'm always a little worried on the streets outside," he said. "Most of the homeless are on drugs. I never thought they'd get inside." He gave her his name; it was almost a mistake. He had two names. One was the name he'd grown up with, the one he thought of as his real self–Buzz. He gave her his business name, reaching across the table and offering his hand, which she took and shook, the look of panic subsiding.

"You think it was a homeless person?" asked the woman.

"I don't know. I guess we probably won't find out until we read it on the web or in tomorrow's papers."

"I'm Julie. Julie Wessenberg," she said, introducing herself. "Do you work in this building?"

"Yes. You?"

"No. I have an appointment at eleven with Bracken and Cherry. They handle my accounts. I own a patisserie on Post Street. We supply many restaurants, including the one in this building."

"I love the croissants here," he said—easy, as he really did like them. "Are they yours?"

"They are."

Looking around, the murderer could see that a calm was settling over the room. The only disturbance was coming from the man who had announced that the elevators had shut down. He was now arguing with the manager of the restaurant. From his table, the murderer could hear only snatches of her reply, but the man was practically shouting at her from a foot away that he had an appointment and couldn't be late. Good, that would be remembered. His talk with Julie about croissants would make a nice contrast, thought the murderer.

It was 11:15 when a policeman entered the restaurant and announced that everyone would be free to go after they answered a few questions. He stood next to the elevators that led to the street level and everyone lined up, the loud man shoving his way to the front. As the line moved forward, the murderer was directly behind Julie Wessenberg. The policeman asked for her ID, took a picture of it on his phone, and asked her a few questions, which he recorded. "Did you hear anything? Did you see a man in a white shirt and khakis with black running shoes? When did you arrive?"

Then it was the murderer's turn. Same questions, and he walked away. Julie had waited for him by the elevators, which still were not working. It looked like they were a couple. They exchanged phone numbers. It couldn't hurt. It was done.

CHAPTER 2

Nate the Great, criminal defense lawyer extraordinaire, driver of a Rolls Royce with the license plate I WIN, phoned me, Rob MacKay. I was just passing the north abutment on the Golden Gate Bridge. It was Wednesday morning. I was on my way to the University of San Francisco. It was just 9 am, early for Nate to call. I put my phone on speaker and placed it on the seat beside me. I promised myself: one more raise and I was getting rid of my 10-year-old Camry. It only had 238,000 miles on it, and both dented doors had been replaced. It was probably good for another ten years, but it was still a ten-year-old Camry.

"Good morning, Nate," I said in my most cheerful voice. I worked for Nate part time as one of his investigators. I knew Nate was unhappy that he hadn't been able to profit by my stint working for Janet Dorrinson the month before. I suspected he thought he might get a client out of the case, but it wasn't to be.

"It sounds like you're driving," said Nate. "Be at my office at 9:30."

"I have some things I have to do at school this morning. Is it important?" As soon as I asked, I knew it was the wrong thing to say. Nate wouldn't have finished his second cup of coffee before making the call.

"Of course it's goddamn important, MacKay," he roared. "Be there."

"Sure," I said. A phone call to D'Jarl Watson, the Senior Associate Basketball Coach and my good friend, would cover for my being late.

Away from legal matters, Nate was a pussycat: polite, funny, and entertaining. But if he was working on a case, he would be a bulldog: short tempered and abrasive. There was no doubt as to which Nate I was dealing with.

I got D'Jarl as he was walking to school from his home in Laurel Heights. "No problem, Rob. When will you be in?"

"I have no clue. Nate isn't one to give details over the phone, only orders."

That got a chuckle from D'Jarl, who had hired Nate when he'd been accused of Rupe Johnstone's murder two years ago. It had never gone to trial, but Nate had prepared a case that would have insured D'Jarl's release if it ever had. Nate had paid for my private investigator's training and license after I helped clear D'Jarl. Now I worked for Nate part time in addition to my real job as the First Assistant Basketball coach at USF.

I decided to park in the lot under Nate's building, paying the outrageous fee. I would give the ticket to his assistant. It was a small act of defiance.

Nate was in the bathroom when I arrived. That meant he'd just come in as well and was taking care of his second cup of coffee. He came out, wiping the residual water off his hands with a paper towel.

"Sit." Yep, Nate was in full form. "I've just got a new client in a murder case, and Mike Ronning is in France on one of those river cruises with his wife for the next two weeks. That makes you my lead investigator." One sentence, three bits of information, without any chance to say anything. Typical Nate the Great in trial mode.

The Janet Dorrinson case had just been solved the month before. I'd helped in the arrest of the killer of three people, including the person who ran the Dorrinson Foundation. I'd allowed myself to get emotionally involved with the victims as well as with Janet Dorrinson, who had hired me. We were still involved, as Janet had asked Michelle, my fiancée, to head her late husband's foundation and Michelle had accepted. They were moving the office to San Francisco, and even though Michelle didn't have to be physically present, she was supervising the move.

"Nate, you know I told Coach Pennington that I wouldn't take any more assignments from you during basketball season."

"If I know my calendar correctly, your fall term doesn't start for another four weeks, and basketball season for another six weeks after that."

"I'm getting married just over a month from now. As far as basketball, I've just been promoted and I'm working hard on bringing in three new recruits. One in particular is taking an extraordinary amount of work and time. Then we're going on a European trip to play three national teams in September. I really don't have the time."

"You only have to do this until Ronning gets back. My son, Norm, is back in town, and I've asked him to help you."

Norm was also an attorney but didn't practice law. We'd gone through high school and then USF as well; he was getting his law degree just as I was earning my graduate degree in business. It would be good working with him again, the only plus I could see in taking this case.

But taking on another case was not fair to Michelle. Ronning's absence put both Nate and me in a difficult spot, I thought.

"Rob, this is a huge case. From what I've already learned, it's pretty open and shut against my client. He swears he's innocent, not that it makes a difference. If I'm going to have a chance at an acquittal, I'm going to need your help. It's important that our investigation starts ASAP."

"When does Mike get back?" I asked.

"September thirteenth." I looked at Nate, adding up the days that Ronning would be away. "He and his wife are visiting Paris and London for a couple days on the way home."

That would take my involvement to just before the team left for Europe. Michelle and Leilah Watson, D'Jarl's wife, were doing most of the wedding planning, but I wanted to add my support. If Michelle was okay with it, then I could help Nate until we left for Europe or Mike Ronning got back. It would also be up to Tip. I'd promised him when he promoted me that basketball would be my first priority.

"If you can work for the next week and a half, I might be able to get Mike to shorten his vacation."

Nate had been good to me. He'd defended me for free during the speed-dating murders, even though he was making big bucks from the Bank of America by representing the parents of the two victims. He'd also put me through PI school and paid all my licensing fees. The jobs that I'd worked for him had added 50% to my coach's salary. This was the first time he had ever asked; he usually just dictated. I was torn, but I knew I owed him.

"Let me talk it over with Michelle. If she's all right with it. I can work till just before the team goes to Europe, but I'll still have to ask for Tip's okay. He's been quite clear that he doesn't want anything interfering with me being a coach."

Nate looked like he was about to explode. "You said that was only during basketball season!"

"Yes, but I've just signed a new contract. I think Tip will agree when I tell him the circumstances. I owe him the courtesy, just like I owe you. Meanwhile, it will be good to work with Norm. What's the case?" I also knew that clearing this with Michelle might be harder than getting Tip's approval.

10

"You might have read this morning that there was a shooting in a lawyer's office in the 560 Mission building yesterday. Two people killed and one injured. They've already arrested my client, Stewart Stemple. He's a financial advisor in the building."

I hadn't heard. "You're going to defend a man accused of killing a lawyer?"

"Everyone is entitled to a defense," said Nate, the rationale I'd heard many times since I started working for him. "And this guy is rich."

Now it made sense.

"I just got the case last night. I'll know soon what they've got that led to such a quick arrest. You clear it with Coach Pennington and he'll be on my list this year. I'm going to the jail to talk to Stemple at 10:30. I'll call you as soon as I know where you should be looking."

That was it. Nate started sifting through the papers on his desk. I was used to his ways. I got up, told his receptionist that I'd text her the parking charge, and left.

CHAPTER 3

I arrived at USF before 10 am. Tip was going to be the first conversation. Michelle would have been, but she was somewhere in the South Bay finishing up at the Dorrinson Foundation's old office and wouldn't be back until dinner time. Neither talk would be easy. One of the negative factors in Michelle taking Janet Dorrinson's offer was that she was now planning two events: the Jonathan Dorrinson Foundation restructuring and move to San Francisco, and our wedding. She was beginning to show the strain. She spent hours each night going over the rules that govern charitable foundations and working out the details of the physical move.

"Good morning, Tip." It seemed as good a way to start as any. "Do you have a minute?" I closed the door to his office and slipped into the chair in front of his desk. Tip Pennington was the long-time head coach of the USF men's basketball team. I'd played for him as an undergraduate, then when I was just starting my master's degree in business, he asked me to join his staff, which was great as it included free tuition. I started as a video coordinator, then moved up year by year to where I was now, his First Assistant.

"Tell me it's something good about Simu," said Tip, looking up from the papers on his desk.

Simu Vuksan was the last recruit we wanted to sign for this coming year: a five star, left handed point guard from Serbia who had only one final hurdle for admission. He wanted to come, and we wanted him–really wanted him. Our other two recruits, D'Andre Blaston Jr., a transfer portal wing from Connecticut, and Booker Oowaite, a freshman center from Oklahoma, were already on campus.

"Nope. Compliance hasn't heard a word about his eligibility."

The NCAA had yet to rule on Simu's playing on a mixed amateur-professional team in Serbia. He needed to be declared an amateur before becoming eligible for a scholarship. The problem was that the NCAA would likely sit on the decision until after the start of the fall semester, thereby making him ineligible to start the year even if they ruled he was eligible at a later date. If that happened, it was likely that Simu would just turn professional.

"What then requires that my door be closed?"

"I'm taking on a short PI job for Nate Hart," I said, thinking it would be best to just get it out.

"Didn't you just finish one?"

"That was for Janet Dorrinson." Tip was the only one besides me who knew that Janet Dorrinson was the anonymous donor of $250,000 to the Hilltop Club, which funded the NIL disbursements to our players. I hoped that the mention of her name might soften his response. It didn't.

"I thought we had agreed that you wouldn't take any more jobs during the season. This technically isn't the season, but we have lots going on with Simu's eligibility still unresolved, Oowaite and Blaston getting acclimated, and our team trip to Europe."

"I know, Tip, but Mr. Hart is in a real bind. He has a big case that desperately needs an investigator, and his main guy is in Europe on a river cruise. Nate needs my help until he gets back. I wouldn't bring this to you unless I thought I could handle it without it interfering with my duties here. Most of it will be in San Francisco, so I won't have to be traveling like I was for Janet Dorrinson."

Tip clearly was not happy. "We've had this conversation before. Remember, you're a basketball coach moonlighting as a private investigator, not the other way around. I still think the time you took away when you were proving D'Jarl's innocence hurt the team. And last year, our players or coaches could have been injured when that guy attacked you during the Pepperdine game."

"Tip, that's not fair. I admit to missing some practices to help D'Jarl, but that was pre-season and I was protecting our player, Damari Murphy, as well. We got to the NCAAs that year and all of our first-string players returned. When has that ever happened? As for last year, it wasn't my fault that someone tried to kill me during the Pepperdine game. The FBI set that up and USF came out smelling like a rose. The guy only had one shot in his dart gun. I was the only one at risk. And again we got to the Sweet 16 in the Show. Hardly a bad season."

"That's true," said Tip. "But you were a Second Assistant then. It's different now that you're First Assistant and if D'Jarl is hired away, like I suspect he will be, you'll be my Associate Head Coach. You'll have less time to play around at being a private investigator. It's time you settled on one career."

"I've told you before that nothing would compromise my duty to you or the team. I know I'm a good basketball coach, but I've proven to be a good investigator as well, and right now Nate Hart needs me until his main investigator gets back. I've handled both jobs before and I'll be able to do it this time. If I find I'm slacking for you or the team in any way, I'll quit the PI job," I said, getting up. I just hoped I could hold true to my promise.

I went back to my office and had hardly sat down when D'Jarl entered.

"What's going on with you? You look bummed."

"I'm taking on a case for Nate, a murder investigation. Mike Ronning is on vacation in Europe and it's put Nate in a bind. I just told Tip and he's not thrilled."

"I can imagine," said D'Jarl. "Is there anything I can do to help? Not with Nate, just if you end up needing a bodyguard around here." D'Jarl, all 6'11" and 250 pounds of him, would make a serious bodyguard. The smile spreading across his face showed that either he was kidding or he was looking forward to pummeling someone who threatened me. I couldn't tell which.

"No, not unless something comes up with the trip that Tip needs help with. Mike Ronning gets back just before we leave for Europe. That will end my involvement. I don't see why I should miss any practices, so the only thing that should require emergency action is Simu Vuksan. I wish there was some way we could speed up the NCAA's decision process. That alone would calm Tip down. And, of course, there's the wedding."

"Would it be okay if I tell Leilah? She's already on the phone with Michelle a couple of times a day."

"Fine, but wait until after 8. I want to talk to Michelle first."

"How's the wedding stuff going?"

"Pretty well. I think I've got all my list done. The girls ask my advice from time to time but they just want me to say yes. Two nights ago Michelle asked me about the color of the centerpieces at the dinner, can you believe it? As if a guy would even notice. She'd made up her mind on that weeks ago."

"I don't see why you're so stressed," said D'Jarl. "You just got Tip upset with you, you're getting married in a month, your number one prospect might turn professional, and you have to investigate a murder. Doesn't our compliance guy, Daly, have a way to push the NCAA's decision on Simu along a little faster? At least that would take one thing off your plate."

"He says no, and he doesn't want me to inquire about it except through him. I think he's more worried about pissing off the NCAA than about what this means to our program."

"I don't know if you've seen the progress Oowaite has made the last couple of weeks. Tip knows the job you did recruiting him and identifying Vuksan, what, three years ago? He'll cut you some slack. What exactly are you doing for Nate?"

"Another murder. His client killed a lawyer and a couple others. Nate's defending a lawyer killer. Can't make him too popular."

"You think Nate cares? Bet the guy is rich." D'Jarl chuckled as he said it.

"Yup," I said. "I'll know more about it later today."

"I'm serious about the bodyguard thing," said D'Jarl. "I've seen the fixes you've gotten yourself into." This time he didn't smile.

My cell phone buzzed. It was Nate. I told D'Jarl. He understood and left.

"I've just seen my client. His name is Stewart Stemple. You go down and talk to him this afternoon. Then come by the office and we'll go over where to start." Nate hung up. No "Can you"? No "Thank you for putting your basketball career on the line." No nothing. I wondered if all lawyers were like Nate.

CHAPTER 4

I'd learned a lot since I started working as a PI for Nate Hart. Heck, I was still learning. One of the things I learned this year was that as an investigator for the attorney of record, I didn't have to sit behind the glass and talk over a phone to the accused. Nate laughed when I told him that I'd done it with D'Jarl. I now knew that I was allowed a private room with the client, no time clock, no phones with bad audio, and no guard breaking up our conversation.

Steward Stemple did not look like a murderer. He looked like the financial advisor that Nate said he was, or maybe even more like an accountant. Even after being in jail for over 24 hours, he somehow appeared well groomed. His hair was combed, and he came into the interview room with a confident stride. I stood and introduced myself as the guard handcuffed him to the table between us.

"Mr. Hart said you would be coming by this afternoon," said Stemple. "I'm to tell you everything that happened."

"That would be great," I said.

"Madison and I were going over some transfers we'd be making later that day when this guy opens the door to my office and…"

"Please, stop right there. I'd like you to start when you entered the building, including the time."

"Sorry." Stemple looked pissed that I had interrupted him. "I get to my office just before 6 am on every day I work. Yesterday

I entered the building at 5:55, went through security, said hello to the guard, took the elevator to the 28th floor, and opened my office. I spent the next two hours checking the market and going over what's happening in Europe and Japan. Sometimes I make trades if the market dictates, but not most days. Most of my accounts are interested in long-term growth, even real estate, not just stocks."

"Was your assistant already there?"

"No. I have Madison, that's Madison Francis, come in at 8 am. She's worked for me for five years–never missed a day. She was responsible for our monthly statements and she provided a buffer between me and my clients when needed. Each morning we would go over the markets, any government legislation that would affect the market, and if my overall strategy had changed for the short or long term. I gave her enough specific details that it usually satisfied the clients. If it didn't, then she routed the call to me. I usually leave at 11 and go to my club, where I play racquetball and take a swim. I have lunch and am back at the office at 1:30 most days for the market close. Wednesday and Friday afternoons I take off and play golf at the club.

"Yesterday, we'd finished our discussion and I was getting ready to leave when my office door slammed open and a man in a ski mask barged in. He seemed confused when he saw Madison. He turned the gun away from me and shot Madison twice without saying a word. She fell bleeding at my feet. He was about to shoot me, but I rushed him and grabbed the gun. We struggled. The gun went off. He pushed me backwards and I tripped over a chair and fell, but I had the gun. He ran toward the exit. I tried to shoot him, but his rifle was empty. I got up and ran after him, but he went into the fire stairwell. He did drop his mask, though. I picked it up and went back to see if I could help Madison. The fire alarm went off. I can't remember if it was before or after I got to Madison. It was horrible. She was such a beautiful, intelligent girl. She was bleeding from shots to her chest and one to her head. I called 911 on my cell, but it just kept ringing. When they finally answered, I told them my assistant had been shot. The lady asked for my location, then said to stay where I was until the police and the medics arrived. I went to my office door and locked it. I was afraid the murderer would return."

"How long was it before the police arrived?" I asked, knowing I could get the time from the police report, or rather Nate could.

"Five or six minutes," said Stemple. "The 911 operator would have the time I called and the police must have a record of when they arrived."

"Did either of you hear any gun shots prior to the man coming into your office?"

"No. If either of us had, we would have locked the office door."

"Why wasn't it locked in the first place?"

"It's always locked at night, of course, and I relock it when I arrive at 6 am. But when Madison arrives at eight, we leave the door open. Anyone coming up to see us has to check in with the ground floor security, and they phone the office for confirmation. It's never been a problem."

"What happened when the police arrived?"

"It was only a couple of minutes after I got in touch with the 911 operator. I heard sirens on the street below. Lots of sirens. A minute later there was pounding on my door and someone shouted 'Police!' I was still afraid that it might be the murderer returning. I went to the door and asked if anyone was with him. Several voices answered, saying 'Officer' and their names. I opened the door. I tried to hand them the gun I'd wrestled from the murderer, but they took one look at me, pointed their own handguns at me, and told me to drop the weapon and hit the floor. I did, and one of them kneeled on my back and handcuffed me. The rest is kind of a blur. They found Madison. I could hear them calling the medics. I kept telling them I was the one who'd called 911 and that Madison was my assistant, but all they did was read me my rights and cart me off downstairs, where I was placed in a police car and driven here. I knew not to say anything more until I talked to an attorney. I remembered Nate Hart from several cases that had been in the paper. I phoned his office and they transferred the call to his cell phone. He saw me this morning and explained that there were other killings three floors above me, but that's all I know."

"The murderer's mask. What happened to it?"

"I put it on Madison's desk when I went back to check on her. I don't know what happened to it after that," said Stemple.

"Did you put it on or put your hand inside it?"

"No, I was careful with it. I only picked it up with two fingers at the very top."

"Do you remember what the murderer was wearing?"

"Well, he wasn't wearing a suit, just a pair of khakis and a white shirt."

"What were you wearing?"

"Like I said, I was ready to go to the club. I had on a pair of khakis, a tee shirt under a button-down collared shirt, no tie, and Nike's."

"Do you own a gun?"

"No, I've never even fired one. I wasn't in the military. They haven't told me–is Madison really dead?"

"I'm afraid so." I watched as Stemple seemed to shrink in front of me. Tears flowed down his cheeks. I gave him a minute to compose himself. I still had questions to ask.

We talked more about his personal life. He wasn't married but he was definitely heterosexual. This might have been his reason for leaving the door to his office open when he was alone with the murdered assistant. He was 44 years old, dated frequently, and had two cars, an Audi S6 sedan and a Mercedes AMG SL 63 Roadster. He might not have any guns, but he had over $300,000 in his garage.

"Were you and your assistant romantically involved?" I asked.

"No. I was very careful about that."

"Never? If you were, it will come out."

"No, never. We had dinner together occasionally, but never anything more than that."

"Did Mr. Hart mention that two other people were shot that morning?"

"Yes, I told him that I didn't know anything about any other victims."

"Did the police ask about them when they questioned you?"

"They asked if I had been to the 32nd floor. I told them no. They were more interested in where I got the gun. I kept quiet after they read me my rights."

"Do you know a woman named Kirsten Grant?"

"No."

"How about Lester Fisher?"

"Was he shot?" asked Stemple, his voice wavering.

"Yes. He's dead," I said, watching him closely.

"He brought a suit against my firm six months ago. He won a small judgement, although he shouldn't have. I resented him, but I wouldn't kill him. It was just money."

To me, Stewart Stemple seemed to be telling the truth. If he was guilty, it might not make a difference to Nate, but it sure would in my work. I was forming an idea as to how I would start my investigation.

"Look, Mr. MacKay. It was my office that was broken into. My assistant was killed and I almost was too. The police should be looking for the murderer, not placing me under arrest. Do something."

"I will," I said. I got up and pressed the button by the door to be let out.

Nate's building was only a mile from the jail. I could have walked it faster than I drove. Again I parked in his building's garage. I took the elevator and was told to go straight into his office.

"Well, what did you think?" asked Nate as I took a seat across from his desk.

"I think he was lucky not to be shot by the police."

"Not that. What do you think of his story?"

"You mean do I think he's telling the truth? I don't know. It would be a great ad lib if he's making it up. The way it came down sure has the case stacked against him."

"Did you ask him what he was wearing?" asked Nate

"Yep. White shirt, no tie, and khakis."

"The guy who shot up the 31st floor was wearing brown pants, a white shirt, and black athletic shoes."

"No wonder they arrested him on the spot," I said. "He came to the door dressed like the murderer, holding the weapon, with a dead woman on the floor behind him and his shirt covered in blood."

"It might help our case that the police acted so quickly if it comes to a trial," said Nate. "Check with Stemple's club and find out if he had a court reserved. It would explain why he was dressed as he was."

"I did find out that the mask he picked up was handled carefully. He only grabbed it at the very top. At least he didn't put it on when he answered the door, holding the gun for the police." It was a snide remark. I thought it was funny. Nate didn't smile.

"We assume he's innocent," said Nate, lecturing me. "The same as we did for D'Jarl Watson. We try to find who did it, or find a straw man, someone else who had motive and opportunity. I only need one juror to side with me to get an acquittal. So start proving Stemple didn't do it or find me an alternative suspect."

"I'd like to start with witnesses to the shooting on the 31st floor," I said. "Try to find any differences in height, weight, clothing, or speech. I imagine you can get a copy of the police report. It would be good to see if it differs from Stemple's account. I'd also like to trace the murderer's path from the 31st floor down to the 28th. Stemple said he followed the guy out into the lobby and he ran into the fire stairs. Where did the murderer go after that?"

"Okay," said Nate. "I'll get the police report and info on the gun. I'll get you access to the crime scene on the 31st floor. Remember to check on any money that could be involved. If it's there, follow it. Anything else?"

"Oh, a biggie," I said. "The lawyer that got killed–he had just sued and won a judgement against Stemple. I don't know the particulars. He didn't know the other woman that was shot. Also, he swears that he had no romantic involvement with Madison Francis, his assistant."

"Yes, he told me that as well. I'll get you access to someone in Fisher's law office. That will give you access to the scene."

So much for taking it easy before the wedding. I decided to spend an hour back at school before going home. There was nothing really pressing, but I thought it might make some repairs to my earlier conversation with Tip.

The basketball offices were almost empty, but on the way in, I passed Tip on his way out. I received a smile and a nod. If I did nothing in the next hour, having Tip see me coming in would have been worth it. I'd just settled in my chair when my cell phone rang. I recognized the Virginia area code but not the number.

"Hello." It was Francis Matobi, Leilah Matobi's, oops, Leilah Watson's father. He was a high-up representative to the United Nations. He was never very clear about what his function was. I knew he had close access to three letter agencies like the FBI and CIA, and I suspected the Secret Service and Homeland Security as well.

"Mr. Matobi. How nice to hear from you." He'd helped me on three different occasions in the last two years. "What can I do for you?"

"I was just talking with D'Jarl and he reminded me that your wedding is coming up soon. I hoped you could provide invitations for two federal employees who will accompany me and Lisa–for the rehearsal dinner, the wedding ceremony, and the dinner. I will gladly pay the added expenses."

"That won't be necessary. I'll tell Michelle tonight. We're so happy that you're coming."

"Wouldn't miss it for the world," said Mr. Matobi. "After all, it was you and Coach Pennington who set me straight on D'Jarl. D'Jarl also mentioned that you were stressed about something at school. Is it anything you can share?"

"It's nothing, really. I've taken a new case for Nate Hart. You'll remember he's the lawyer who defended D'Jarl. Coach Pennington wasn't exactly thrilled. He's worried about a five-star recruit from Serbia not being handled correctly. The NCAA is holding up ruling on his eligibility. We're afraid if they don't rule before the beginning of fall semester, the kid will go pro."

"That's good news," chuckled Mr. Matobi. "Lisa was worried that you were concerned about the wedding."

"Nope. I'll let Michelle know about the two extra guests. It won't be a problem. I'm sure she'll have Leilah let you know it's okay." We said our goodbyes and clicked off.

I checked in with Michelle. If I left now, I could pick up Jenny's Chinese and still be home before her. Jenny's was easy; they had my order down pat. Lemon chicken for Michelle, Mongolian beef for me, with fried rice and pot stickers. To be sure that Michelle would be more than just pleased, I added green beans and asparagus with almonds. I wouldn't touch it, but Michelle would be happy to have it to herself.

CHAPTER 5

When Michelle arrived, I'd already set the table. By the time it took her to take off her work clothes, freshen up, and climb into her designer sweats, I'd served the food and poured her a glass of wine, a non-alcoholic beer for me. She looked tired.

"Is this new job going to be too stressful?" I asked. We hadn't been intimate in a week. I was also feeling guilty that I wasn't doing as much as she was for the wedding.

"No, not at all. Once we get the new office set up, it will be a lot less work than the store was. I'll also be home at a decent time. It's just the move and the wedding being so close together. It couldn't be avoided, as the Foundation's lease in Palo Alto is about to expire. The move is simple. Just computers and furniture. What's taking the time is arranging the infrastructure of the new space and setting up the utilities and internet along with security. You can't believe the security. Janet wants it twice as strong as before."

"Speaking of security, Mr. Matobi called me today and asked if we could add two guests to all the functions. I suspect they are his bodyguards. I noticed them at Leilah's wedding–two guys, no dates, dark glasses. If it's all right with you, I'll phone the club and add them to our number."

"How sweet," she said, spooning a load of the asparagus onto her plate.

I was unsure if I was sweet because of the offer to call the club or for getting the asparagus. It didn't matter. She'd brightened up.

"Something's come up for me as well. Nate has put me on another case."

Michelle looked up. Her whole expression changed. "So close to our wedding? Plus, you're going overseas with the team soon. Isn't that a little inconsiderate?"

It took a few minutes to tell her about Nate's problem with Mike Ronning and the case. She was somewhat relieved that I had given him a two-week drop-dead time for my involvement, but she was still upset. We ate the rest of the meal in relative quiet and went to bed early. I gave her a back massage and scratch. She was grateful, but that was as intimate as we got. Before I finished the back scratch, she was gently snoring.

We had gone to bed so early that both of us woke up before the alarm. Sun was piercing the cracks between the window slats. It was one of the things I still had to fix. We were just getting used to our new bedroom, which a month ago had been a garage. Michelle had all but converted my office into a spare bedroom as well, so we now had two guest rooms. They would both be filled a lot of the time from now through our wedding. I was really beginning to worry about having only a single bathroom. I checked the time; it was half an hour before the alarm would have woken us.

"Thank you for the back scratch," said Michelle. "I don't remember much after you started."

"You were snoozing before I stopped. Did you sleep well?"

"I feel great." She took a quick look at the time and proceeded to show her appreciation. Half an hour later, I felt well thanked. We were both lying on our backs recovering our breath when the alarm rang.

—

I smiled all the way across the Golden Gate Bridge. I hoped I'd made Michelle's day start as pleasantly as mine. I reminded myself that Michelle should always be the most important thing in my life. Being a basketball coach was important, but not as much as our wedding. Nate's job was further down the list. I pulled into the school parking lot still smiling.

D'Jarl was already in his office when I passed by.

"Anything new on the status of Simu Vuksan?" he asked when he saw me.

"Still the same."

"I was about to call Weston Daly in compliance and ask about NIL money," said D'Jarl, picking up the desk phone and dialing.

"Weston, can NIL money be given to a walk-on in basketball?" Basketball was considered a counting sport, which meant that the NCAA allowed enough full scholarships, 14, to field a full team. Tip liked to carry 16 players, as there always seemed to be three or four with injuries. The extra two non-scholarship players were called walk-ons. While we couldn't split scholarships, we might be able to get around the issue by giving them NIL money. It was the reason for the question.

"I think so. Let me find out for sure." He hung up.

"That was interesting," I said.

D'Jarl's phone rang. It was Daly. He clicked it on speaker phone so I could hear.

"That didn't take long," said D'Jarl.

"I guess it's a question they've been getting a lot lately," said Weston. "Yes, a walk-on can receive NIL money. The NCAA isn't happy about it because it essentially removes all scholarship limitation numbers from their control. But in the Vuksan case, you definitely can't offer him NIL money until he's fully admitted."

"Let's go see Tip," said D'Jarl as he hung up.

The door was open. I still knocked before we entered Tip's office. One look at us and he waved us in.

"Have a seat. What do you have for me?"

"I just got some clarification from compliance. Any person on a team is eligible for NIL money, even a walk-on."

"Interesting," said Tip. "How much NIL money is left?"

"I checked with Matt Horsay a few months ago. We had $84,000, but Matt wanted to keep $30,000 in reserve."

"In Simu's case he has to wait until he's admitted to get a guarantee of an NIL offer," said D'Jarl. "He still has to get the NCAA's okay on him having amateur status, something that we have no control over."

D'Jarl was right. The matter was out of our control, except that I was sure a conversation with Janet Dorrinson could very well increase the NIL account, enough to satisfy Simu and his parents.

There was still enough time to phone Coach Jovanovic and tell him about the NIL ruling. We left to go to D'Jarl's office, where I phoned Serbia on my cell phone.

"Beabet." There was that word again. It had to mean something like "Hello." I made a mental note to ask Bogdan about it. "Coach MacKee."

"I have some news, Coach. Simu can get NIL money legally as long as he's on the team, even as a walk-on with no scholarship."

"That is goot news," said Jovanovic.

"He still has to pass the TOEFL and get clearance from the NCAA. He can't be on the team even as a walk-on until that happens, and I've just heard that the NCAA won't rule until sometime in October."

"That will be hard. Simu go pro if he not certain of joining your team."

"Ivo," said D'Jarl. "It's D'Jarl Watson."

"Ah, Coach Watson. Nice hear you."

"Ivo, these things have a way of working out. Just get Simu to take the TOEFL. That's important. We still have two months for the rest. Is Bogdan happy with the way I'm coaching him?"

I could tell that D'Jarl wanted to get off the possibility of Simu turning pro. D'Jarl had gone pro early. He was wealthy because of his decision but was taking courses at night to earn his degree. D'Jarl was making up for something he'd missed–not so much his youth, but perhaps being labeled a jock and nothing more. It had almost cost him Leilah's parents' approval for his marriage to their daughter.

"He says you tough, not as tough as me, but you show him footwork and shots that I haven't. You do goot job with him. He much improved."

We said our goodbyes and hung up. D'Jarl and I discussed what we had learned in the last few minutes, then switched to other things: the upcoming European trip and the wedding. I was about to tell him more about the new case I'd taken on for Nate when my cell phone rang. It was Nate. I left D'Jarl's room and took the call. Nate wanted to see me at his office before noon. For once, I wouldn't be rushed.

Nate handed me a stack of papers as I entered his office. "This is the judge's decision on the suit that Fisher filed against Stewart Stemple's company. Also, I've talked with a lawyer in Fisher's firm this morning. He was in the area when Fisher and Kirsten Grant were killed. He's willing to talk with you, but the firm has sent a directive to all employees that any questions about the shooting should be referred to the operating partner. They're trying to keep a tight lid on this, and I don't blame them."

"How am I going to talk to him?" I asked, looking at the name on the sheet of paper. It read Franklin Whistel. I thought it was good that he had Frank as a first name because he certainly would have been kidded in school about Whistel.

"You've got an appointment to meet with him at 560 Mission at 1:30 this afternoon on a legal matter. You'll have a private room. He knows what you really want to talk about. I thought that it would be good to not only talk with him but also see the scene of the murder, although Frank says that much of it is still taped off."

I was sure that Nate was paying Whistel the normal consultation fee as well as a substantial "gift" for the interview. "Did you see or talk to Stemple this morning?" I asked.

"No, he's not my only case. I have several that I'm finishing up. It's one reason that it's so important for you to replace Mike on this one. The preliminary police report is also in there." Nate waved at the papers he'd handed me. "We're not supposed to have it but there's lots of important information in it."

"Such as?" I asked.

"Such as the gun, an Uzi, is a real ghost gun. No serial number, no record anywhere. Same with its 25-shot stock. Only two floors, the 31st and the 28th, had their doors jimmied. My source says it would have taken some expertise and time to rig them the way they were done. The only other way out of that fire escape stairwell was the door that emptied into the lobby. Read it for yourself." Nate was through. I knew the sign and left.

I had time to visit Stewart Stemple before seeing Whistel. I left my car in Nate's garage and walked the ten blocks to the jail.

It took twenty minutes to get into the interview room with Stemple. Obviously lunchtime was not the best time to visit the jail.

Two days in jail hadn't taken anything away from Stemple's "I'm the smartest guy in the room" personality. "What has Hart been doing?" he asked.

"Working on some leads," I said. I saw no reason not to tell him all of what Nate had shared about his defense. "I'm trying to identify the person who killed Fisher and Madison Francis. At the same time, I'm looking for alternative suspects who might have had a grudge against Fisher. If this goes to trial, Nate will want someone to deflect blame away from you. Right now you're the police's only person of interest."

"Muddying the water isn't proving me innocent."

"No, it isn't," I agreed. "But it's a heck of a lot better than spending the next half of your life on death row. It's worth stirring the bottom a bit. Let me ask you a few questions. What color shoes were you wearing?"

"Black Nikes. I always wear them on days I play racquetball. Look, the police have them. They took them when they gave me this classic outfit."

That was not good. It was the same color the shooter had worn. I didn't tell Stemple, though. That would be up to Nate.

"Is there anything else you've thought of?" I asked.

"Yeah. I wish the gun hadn't been empty and I'd shot the son of a bitch."

I looked at the clock on the wall. I had an appointment to keep just down the street at 560 Mission with a guy named Whistel.

CHAPTER 6

I didn't know how strong security had been in the lobby of 560 Mission on the day of the shootings, but it was full bore now. I noted cameras in at least three locations. A man in a gray suit entered in front of me with credentials and still had to go through the metal detector and have his badge scanned. All I had was an appointment set up by Nate with Franklin Whistel. I explained that to the first guard, went through the metal detector, and was stopped by the second guard, who wanted to see my driver's license, then used the phone to call the offices of Braddock, Fisher, and Bunting. The appointment was confirmed. My driver's license returned, I went to the bank of elevators. They were modern, they were fast, they were quiet, and I was alone. The doors opened on the 31st floor with a soft ping.

In front of me was a receptionist desk with an extremely attractive woman sitting behind it. In back of her was an open floor plan with cubicles for the dozens of people working there. The only enclosed offices were arranged against the outside walls with glass separating their occupants from those in the front. There was yellow police tape securing a good third of the area to the back and right of the receptionist.

"I have an appointment with Mr. Whistel," I said. "Robert MacKay."

The lady behind the desk looked at me. I thought the way she did it was a little too critical. She punched a few keys on her desk phone and said, "Mr. MacKay to see you," into the small microphone that hovered like a bee above her perfectly applied lipstick.

The individual who rose and made his way to the front could only have been Franklin Whistel. He was more a Whistel than he was a Frank. He was balding, a fact made more evident than it should have been due to his height, which couldn't have been more than 5' 6". Despite those limitations, he looked friendly, with an open face and a good smile. It was his eyes that dominated his features. They were light brown and gentle, reminding me of a puppy dog.

"Robert," he said, extending his hand. "Nice to meet you."

The receptionist shot me another look as Whistel guided me to an unoccupied office in the back. He closed the door behind us and we sat at 90 degrees to each other at the head of a large table.

"I don't know if Nate told you but no one is allowed on this floor without an appointment. We couldn't just shut down our entire firm for however long it takes the police to finish their investigation. I have a file for you in case anyone asks. No one is supposed to talk about the shooting."

"That's fine. What area of law do you practice?"

"I handle the divorce cases for the firm," said Whistel. Now the nasty looks I'd received from the receptionist made sense. "We're primarily a business law firm, but many of our clients are quite well off and want to keep their divorces in house. It helps in protecting certain of their assets."

"We have a problem then. I'm not married."

Whistel's puppy dog eyes looked like I'd just kicked him. Then they brightened. "Are you going out with someone?"

"Yes. In fact, I'm to be married on September 28th."

"Good, good. Then we're discussing a prenuptial agreement." He fanned open a yellow legal pad.

In the next five minutes I gave him more information about me and Michelle than I was comfortable supplying.

"I've got enough to explain your appointment," said Whistel, looking up from his pad. "What is it you want to know about the shooting?"

"Where were you when it happened?"

"I was at my desk on the phone." He nodded to his right at an area a good distance from where the yellow tape was. "I didn't see him come in, but he fired a number of shots and I ducked under my desk. Lawyers know it's always a possibility that someone holds a grudge."

"So you didn't see him?"

"I looked up for an instant when Kirsten Grant started screaming. The gunman was in Mr. Fisher's office by then. When he came out, I saw him, but I ducked under my desk again. He fired two more shots. I thought he was shooting at me. I was still on the phone. I think everyone in the office was dialing 911. Someone shouted 'He's gone,' and I peeked around my desk and saw people moving. Kirsten was still screaming."

"How many were in the office?"

"Thirty-four including Mr. Fisher and Kirsten."

"Can you describe the shooter?"

"He was wearing a black knit mask with a red slash across the front. White shirt and, I think, brown pants, but I'm not sure. I didn't raise my head high enough to see much of his legs."

"Do you have security cameras in the office?"

"No." Whistel looked at me as if I was crazy. "Not likely in an attorney firm."

"Who in the office got a good look at the gunman?"

Whistel gave me the names of two others who'd given descriptions of the man to the police. One was the receptionist.

"Did Mr. Fisher have any enemies here in the office, or any-where else that you know of?"

Whistel broke into a grin. "Enemies? I take it you didn't know Lester Fisher?"

"No, enlighten me."

Whistel looked at me like he was explaining the ABC's. "I guess you wouldn't know, working for Hart. He's a criminal attorney. He's always going up against public defenders, and criminal lawyers and public defenders are seldom on good terms. In a business law office, most of our cases settle. For the most part, both parties are satisfied. Even in my cases, I might paint the opposing attorney as Satan reincarnated to my client. It's good practice to have them dislike the opposing lawyer as much as their ex-spouse. It drives up the hours and makes compromise harder, but after the final judgement, it's not unusual for me to go out with the opposing attorney and have drinks. It's the same in civil cases. It's just the business of law."

"And Fisher?"

"Lester Fisher was different. He didn't want compromises, he wanted total annihilation. Needless to say, he did not go out for drinks with his opposition."

"How about inside the firm?"

"The same," said Whistel. "He was very critical of anyone who didn't get what he thought was the maximum judgment."

"Did that include you?"

"Particularly me. He felt that if I was representing a man, his ex-spouse should end up standing on a street corner with a card-board sign reading 'PLEASE HELP.' No judge was ever going to allow that, even if it were my goal."

I was getting a pretty clear picture of Lester Fisher. I'd ask Nate for his opinion and if he had ever crossed swords with him.

I'd need a list of suits that he was involved in over the last year to make a list of people who would wish him harm.

"Could you walk me to the front? Get as near as possible to the taped-off areas. How long would it normally take to write a pre-nup?"

"It depends on how much one has to protect," said Whistel. "A couple of days on the average, but I can stretch if to a week."

"Fine. Let's make an appointment while we walk through the office."

I wanted to see where the shooting took place, then go down the fire escape door instead of using the elevator. Franklin Whistel could have been a fine actor if he hadn't turned to law. As we walked through the office, he asked about my house and school retirement plan. We made an appointment for 10 am the day after tomorrow. He promised to have a rough draft.

"Thank you for your help," I said as we passed the reception-ist. "You make it sound simple. I still have time to get in my steps before I have to return to work."

As I neared the bank of elevators, I heard Whistel tell the receptionist to schedule a second pre-nup appointment for my impending wedding. Maybe she wouldn't be giving me the death stare treatment now that she knew I wasn't getting a divorce. She noted the appointment, smiling a rehearsed smile while putting something into the computer on her desk. Regardless, it dis-tracted her enough for me to get to the fire escape door, which was unlocked from inside by regulations, and slip through. An alarm went off as the door clicked shut behind me. I tried the handle but it was locked. The stairwell was poorly lit and had none of the expensive features of the rest of the building. It was basic concrete stairs with a banister made of pipe. I tried every door as I passed. They were all locked. I made a mental note to bring a strong flashlight if I ever did this again. The police report had said that only the 31st and 28th floor doors had been tampered with. If so, where had the murderer gone? How had he gotten out of the stairwell? There were only a few possibilities, I thought. He could have slipped back in and remained on the two floors, or he could have left at the ground floor like I was doing.

The ground floor door was free to open. It had taken me five minutes to go down the 30 flights of stairs. I'd gone fast, taking the steps two at a time, but I'd stopped at every landing, trying the doors, so the murderer could have made it faster. Standing on the other side was one of the security guards I'd passed in the lobby entry on the way up. He was not happy.

"What do you think you're doing?" he asked, putting up a hand for me to stop. His other hand was on the gun that was still in its holster on his hip.

"Just trying to get my steps in," I said. "I tried to go back, but the door was locked. It's really dark in there. You ought to put in some better lighting."

"That's only for use in the case of fire."

"Sorry, I didn't realize that. Nobody said anything when I left Mr. Whistel's office."

The guard had me stand by his desk while he phoned the 31st floor. He scanned my driver's license, then had me walk through the security scanner again. Finally I was free to leave.

I was only half kidding about my steps. I tried to run at least fifteen miles every week. That and basketball practices were enough to keep me fit, but as I was now 31 years old, I was gaining a little weight. This was why I had left my car at Nate's garage and walked to the jail, then to the law offices. Now I walked back to Nate's. I was appalled at the conditions south of Market. Homeless tents and shopping carts filled with belongings were to be seen on

38

every block. It was better as I crossed Market Street to the financial district, but I had the feeling that in a few years it would be the same there as well.

The housing shortage and homelessness problems were hampered by San Francisco's supervisors, who were elected by district. All of them were pro housing and all for helping the unhoused–just not in their own districts. That combined with a Machiavellian set of overlapping housing regulations resulted in lots of money being spent in committees and almost nothing getting done. San Francisco used to be known as the "How To City," but that was when the supervisors were elected city wide, not by district.

I really didn't have a lot to tell Nate. I could call him with my request for a list of judgments that Fisher had been involved in. I'm sure he was aware of Fisher's reputation. There would be no dearth of alternative suspects. The problem was the evidence against Stemple being so strong. I got to my car and drove to school.

I was just settling in when my cell rang. I was surprised that it was an international call. I looked at the clock on the wall. It would be midnight in Serbia.

"Coach MacKee," came the greeting. "Goot news. Simu will be taking TOEFL in two days, in Paris. He fly there tomorrow."

I was not sure that this was such a good idea. Coach Jovanovic had mentioned that Simu was taking an English class. From the way he spoke when he visited, I thought he needed a lot of help before he took the test. His English was nowhere near as good as Bogdan's was when he entered. I hoped he wasn't jumping the gun. Poor choice of words, I thought, thinking of Stewart Stemple.

CHAPTER 7

I had just hung up after talking with Coach Jovanovic when my cell phone rang. The ID showed that it was Norm Hart, Nate's son.

"Hey, Rob. Nate tells me you need help on a case?" In a few ways Norm was like his father. In most ways, he was completely different. He'd gone to law school but never practiced law. We'd been best friends since high school. He'd helped clear me of the speed-dating murders. Soon after that he'd left the area, and I hadn't heard from him in nearly two years.

"Norm, good to hear from you. Your dad said you might help me until his main investigator gets back."

"I'd hoped to sneak into town and out before Nate found anything for me to do. I didn't make it," said Norm. "Where are you now?"

"I'm at school."

"Great, I'll drop by in an hour or so."

"We've moved offices." I told him to call and I'd meet him in front of the gym. "Can you get access to all the judgments Lester Fisher has been involved with in the past year? I asked Nate, but you're a lawyer too."

"Shouldn't be hard. Give me another half hour."

I spent the next 45 minutes reviewing the suit Fisher had filed against Stewart Stemple's company. It resulted in the loss of almost a million dollars in judgments and penalties. Stemple had said that it was just money, it was only business. If a million dollars didn't provide a motive, I didn't know what would.

Norm showed up almost half an hour late with his lawyer's briefcase filled with files. He was tan and very fit. His hair had always been curly and cut short. Now the tight curls hung just above his collar. It was good to see him.

As much as I had to get down to the business of helping Stewart Stemple, Norm's friendship came first.

"You look great," I said. "What the heck have you been doing the last couple of years?"

"It was part of the deal that Nate and I worked out," said Norm. "He insisted that I go to law school. I didn't want to. We agreed that if I went and then passed the Bar, he would finance me for two years while I did whatever I wanted. No questions asked."

"So what did you do? I never even got to thank you for helping me with the speed- dating murders."

"I started with the usual. France, Italy, but got tired of being a tourist. Spent three months on Majorca, got island fever, and went to India. That's where I've been for the last year."

"And now you're back?"

"For a little while. Nate has always wanted me to go into practice with him. It's not something I'm ever going to do. I don't like practicing law, particularly criminal law."

I remembered that Norm had said much the same thing when I'd asked him to represent me in the speed-dating murders. He'd referred me to his dad, saying that he was a lawyer but didn't practice law.

"I glad you're going to help me," I said, meaning it. "I'm up against it timewise and can really use the help."

"Nate said you were in a bind."

"It's the other way around. Nate's in a bind. He took a case that he's likely to lose." I took the better part of the hour outlining the case against Stemple and explaining Mike Ronning's absence.

"I don't know why Nate took the case," I said. "Stemple has money to pay him, but I don't see how he's going to win it. The police found Stemple with the murder weapon, his prints all over it, including the trigger. He had powder evidence on him. His description matched the killer's, and he had the mask that the murderer was wearing. He was in the building only three floors down. The reentry mechanism on his fire door had been tampered with, as had the one on the 31st floor where Lester Fisher was shot. Add to it that Fisher had just won a big judgement against Stemple, and you have the trifecta. Stemple had motive, opportunity, and the ability to do in Fisher. Two dead, one injured, and Stemple swears he's innocent."

"What does Nate have you doing?" asked Norm.

"The usual. Trying to find evidence that would prove Stemple's innocence, or ways of discrediting the evidence against him. Short of that, finding someone else who had motive and opportunity. Someone Nate can use as an alternative to create doubt in the jury's mind. He says he only needs one juror to have reasonable doubt to get a hung jury."

"That would be Nate all right," said Norm. "So where do we start?"

"We still don't have all the evidence the police have. I'm sure Nate will get it soon in discovery, though. What we do know already is enough for the DA to get a conviction. Until we find out their entire case, I thought it would be best to look for a straw man. That's why I asked for those judgments," I said, pointing at Norm's briefcase.

"Let's get to it then," said Norm. He pulled out a fistful of documents.

"Wow," said Norm as we finished going over the last of the judgments. "This guy Fisher was a real piece of work."

"You're right about that. All but two of those thirteen cases would give us someone who held a grudge. It doesn't do anything to lessen the evidence against Stemple, however. It's so strong that no matter how many other people would have liked to knock Fisher off, it won't matter."

"Rob," said Norm. "Remember when we were in high school? In chemistry, everyone wanted you to help them identify their unknown sample. You're really good at solving things. So what do we do next?"

"Check with the eleven who were screwed by Fisher and see if they have an alibi for 10 to 11 am on the day of the murder."

"I can do that," said Norm.

It felt like we were moving ahead, or at least in some direction.

I still had half an hour before I normally left school. I spent it checking my messages. Nothing from Simu or Coach Jovanovic. Nothing from compliance, not even anything from Tip. I checked the emails from prospects; knowing that we were finished with our recruiting made replies easier. We had a form "Sorry, No Room" letter. I only had to type a name at the top and hit send. My mind kept going back to the case. Stemple had reason enough to kill Fisher, but the outlier was Madison Francis, his assistant. Why was she killed? I stuck it away in the pocket of my brain that held unanswered questions and got up to go home.

—

I had time, so I stopped at the grocery store just down the street from school on Fulton and bought a filet of salmon and some fresh snow peas. We already had rice at home. It would take the longest to cook. I would barbecue the salmon, and the peas were so fresh they could be eaten raw.

Michelle came in while I was lighting the barbeque grill in the backyard. She looked happy, not nearly as tired as the day before.

"Table set, with flowers. Rice cooking. What are you getting ready to grill?"

"Salmon. Would you turn on the snow peas?"

"My, my. Remind me to wake up a half hour early more often," said Michelle, turning back to the kitchen with a mischievous grin.

The salmon took only a few minutes. I cooked it on a thin cedar plank and managed not to overdo it. The snow peas were just beginning to boil when I brought the fish in from the back yard. I served the meal with a dill sauce and we sat down.

"The new space is finished. We could move in tomorrow," said Michelle. "You can't imagine what a load off me that is. The move itself will be nothing. The staff is almost as happy as I am."

"That's great news. I have some too. Norm Hart is back in town. Nate has asked him to help me with the new case. It looks like he's going to be around for a while. I was wondering if you would mind another wedding guest?"

"You realize what each guest costs, don't you?" said Michelle, her temper rising. "You know we're trying to keep the costs down, but you keep adding guests. You're not going to ask him to be in the wedding party, are you?"

"Nope. Just a guest. Maybe if he'd come back a few months ago, but things are too far along. I had no idea that Norm would be in town until yesterday. Mr. Matobi offered to cover the cost of his two security men. I told him we'd take care of them."

"Still, please don't invite anyone else," said Michelle, with more understanding in her voice. "Things are getting a little crazy."

"Things got a little crazy at school today as well. I forgot to phone the club to add the two security guys. If it's all right, I'll add Norm and do it tomorrow."

"I'm sorry I jumped on you." Michelle laughed. She got up and kissed me full on the lips. "My turn to clean up."

We spent half an hour in the front room talking about all that had been done at Michelle's office to get the space ready for the move and a little about her staff. I'd already met them. I'd questioned them when Sue Brascco, their previous boss, had gone missing. I told Michelle a bit about the case Nate had given me. Mostly I told her how bleak it was for the guy Nate was representing. We went to bed knowing that while things might have gotten better, there was still a lot on both our plates.

Since we'd moved into our new offices above the practice court, some of our old ones hadn't been reassigned. One in particular was still empty and was perfect for Norm. I asked Tip if I might have the use of it for the two weeks that I'd given Nate. I would let Norm use it for his work space since he had no desire to use his father's office. We could also have our meetings there and not interrupt anything that was going on with the other coaches. The office had windows to the outside so there was good internet and cell service. Tip gave his okay but only for the two weeks.

———

Norm was settled in by noon. He gave me a call at 2 pm. He wanted to go over the eleven cases that Lester Fisher had closed in the previous year.

"What an asshole this guy was!" said Norm as I entered. "He must have cherry picked his cases, taking the ones that were sure wins, but also ones where he could punish the opposition."

"I take it you've identified the individuals he screwed over?"

"Yeah. Eight of the eleven have solid alibis. I'll still check them out. One guy I haven't found, and two don't have anyone to vouch for their whereabouts."

"You've gotten a lot done. What's with the missing one?"

"Who knows? He could be in a homeless shelter after what Fisher did to him. Brutal."

"Well, check the alibis. You know what Nate would say about it if you didn't. Also, see if any of the others fit the description of the murderer: 5'10"–5'11" or so, normal build, maybe 170 pounds. Check and see if they had any weapons training. If we can't connect them with location, maybe we can with another trait. Keep picking at it. I have to go to the jail and see Stemple again. There's something about the death of his assistant that doesn't add up."

I realized that Michelle's new digs were just a few blocks away from 560 Mission, just off Market on 3rd Street. I was tempted to drop by, but I was cutting it close visiting Stemple as it was. Same routine, same conference room, same Stemple handcuffed to the table in front of me. The only difference was that Stemple had lost much of his cockiness. Jail was having its effect.

"Did you see the killer enter from the fire stairwell?" I asked as soon as he was settled.

"No, our door to the lobby was closed. I told you that. But he left that way. I saw him before I went back to try and help Madison."

"That's right, closed but not locked."

"I don't remember hearing an elevator ding before he barged in, though," said Stemple. "Usually we're attuned to that."

"So the guy enters. He doesn't say a word, and he shoots Madison twice, killing her. Why didn't he shoot you? I would have thought you were the bigger threat."

"I don't know. He had the gun aimed at me. Madison wasn't in his way or anything. It was like he was surprised to see her. After he shot her, he had at least one bullet left. I think that was for me. That's when I jumped him."

"That's right–you struggled for the gun, and Madison was shot again."

"Right. He pulled the trigger, though. I had hold of the barrel. It was hot."

"What happened then?"

"We went over this," said Stemple, losing what was left of his cool.

"Yes, but again, please."

"I wrestled the gun away from him and he panicked and ran toward the door. I fired the gun, trying to shoot him, but it was empty. I ran after him in time to see him leaving by the fire stairs. He'd dropped his mask on the way out."

The police report stated that 14 shots were used on the 31st floor. Three more were used, killing Madison Francis. That made 17 total. The clip could hold 25 bullets. What happened to the other eight? Something didn't add up, I thought. This murder was premeditated and well thought out. The tampering with the door locks proved that. If so, why wasn't the clip full?

"So you saw the back of his head. Was he blond, red-headed?"

"I don't know. I only saw him for a brief second as the door closed. It was dark in the stairwell." Stemple thought for a moment. "Black. The back of his head was black, the same color as the mask. Look, I'm innocent. I didn't shoot anyone."

Methinks he doth protest too much, ran through my mind. I knew it was 'She doth,' not 'Stemple doth,' but the quote seemed to fit. Why would the man who had planned out the murder of Fisher so meticulously panic? Nate had said, "Think of Stemple as innocent." If he was, there was a lot that didn't line up.

"All right," I said. "Like I told you yesterday, Nate is going at this two pronged. He's trying to prove you are innocent, but barring that, he's looking for others who had reason to want to hurt Fisher. It's Madison I can't figure out, and why the murderer ended up in your office in the first place. So by tomorrow, I want you to compile a list of people who would like to harm you."

"Harm me?"

"Yes, get even for something you've done. You're a financial advisor. You must have had a bad account or two. Make a list of all you can remember. It's a long shot, but it gives Nate another bullet to use." I immediately regretted my choice of words. I slid a legal pad and a pen over to Stemple and rang the buzzer for the guard.

I called Michelle as I left the jail and agreed to meet her for dinner at Jenny's. We ordered takeout so often, it would be good to eat out for a change–almost like a date.

CHAPTER 8

As soon as I passed through the Robin Williams tunnel, I called the Meadow Club and added three to the guest list for the wedding dinner, two for the rehearsal dinner. As Michelle had found, working with the event manager at the club was a pleasure.

It had been a while since we had eaten at Jenny's, and Jenny's daughter, Lin, treated us like royalty, fussing over the table and chatting with Michelle about the wedding. She had gotten married a year before and we'd been invited. Michelle had insisted that Lin get an invite to ours. I bit my tongue about her getting mad at me for adding Norm. I sat there while the two women shared experiences. When the food came, we took our time eating. Michelle told me about her day. The entire office was packed up. Tomorrow it would be moved to the new foundation space in San Francisco. Michelle thought it would be harder to unpack and set up all the computers than it had been to pack them, but that they would be up and running the day after tomorrow.

For my part, I told her about my second interview with Stemple and my confusion over the killing of Madison Francis; her being shot three times didn't fit with Kirsten Grant having only been shot in the leg. There was another question that had entered my mind as well. Why did the murderer take off his mask when he did? There were things that didn't add up. I didn't have enough to make Nate's case any easier, just enough to make my own job harder.

"When I get the foundation settled in, would you like me to help you like I did with your other cases?"

"I don't think it'll be necessary. I've got Norm checking on alibis for others who might want Fisher dead." I knew that Michelle still had scads of work to do not only setting up the office but also learning the rules that govern charitable foundations. And then there was our wedding.

"Okay, but I'd still like to know what you uncover. It seems odd that Nate would take the case. It seems so open and shut."

"Money," I said. It was the only explanation that fit.

I received a surprise when I got to school the next day. Winfred Ramsey, our Director of Compliance, had left a message on my house phone to call him, which I did.

"Good news," he said. As Director of Compliance, unlike the coaches, Ramsey had a 9 to 5 job. "I just got Simu Vuksan's TOEFL exam results–97. Admissions says they can work with that."

I was amazed. Simu had gotten almost the same test results as Bogdan. The requirement had gone from a stumbling block to his admission to a plus factor in his favor. I was thanking Ramsey for letting me know when my cell rang. It was Coach Jovanovic.

"Coach MacKee," came the now familiar greeting. "Good news. Simu just got results of the English test. He pass with 97."

"We just received that news as well from the testing agency. That score makes him eligible for admission." It was a big deal. There were other schools that didn't worry about an applicant being able to speak English, particularly if he was an athlete. Eight years before, the men's golf coach had recruited a Spanish kid. His TOEFL was short by ten points for our admissions. Arizona State had no such qualms. He went there, became the number one amateur in the nation, went professional, and now led the professional golf rankings, having won two Majors in the space of seven years. He would have been a game changer for our program, and he now spoke perfect English.

"I tell you no problem," said Jovanovic.

"Now we have to get the NCAA to rule that he's still an amateur, but it's likely to be a long time coming."

"He still amateur. You will see." We said our goodbyes.

I'd only been at school for 15 minutes and a major worry had already been taken away. This was starting to be a very good day.

The whole team would be at school in three days, preparing and practicing for the European trip against the national teams of Spain, France, and Sweden. Our new players, Booker Oowaite and D'Andre Blaston, were already in school, taking summer courses. Only Simu Vuksan's situation was unresolved.

I'd forgotten about Norm. It was still early, but I thought I'd check on him. He was in, and it looked like he'd been there for a while.

"I was just going to get a cup of coffee," I said as I entered the small space that he was using as a temporary office. "Would you like me to bring you one?"

"I'll go with you," said Norm, closing his laptop. "I haven't had breakfast yet."

The school cafeteria wasn't open fully, but it had enough to do the job with bagels, doughnuts, and cereal. We sat while Norm finished two bagels with about three-quarters of an inch of cream cheese on top.

"Bad news on the guy I couldn't find. He was in Nebraska. That leaves only two possible candidates, and they don't look too good. Neither one fits your description of the murderer. I thought I would check out Fisher's current cases as well. It might be a little harder since none of them have court rulings yet. Do you have anyone inside the firm I could talk to?"

"Your dad gave me a contact. I've talked with him already and he was quite cooperative." I gave him Franklin Whistel's number. "I've also asked Stemple who might have a grudge against him. It's a long shot, but we don't seem to be getting anywhere with the list of Fisher's enemies."

"That should be interesting. A finance guy snitching on himself for dirty deeds done," said Norm, shaking his head as he forced the last bite of bagel into his mouth.

"Assume that Stemple is telling the truth and is innocent of all the shootings," I said. "Then there are things that don't make sense."

Norm looked up and gave me a "Continue" expression, his eyebrows raised.

"Nate's informant in the police says that the only two fire escape doors that were tampered with were the ones on the 31st and 28th floors. The killer could have entered anywhere, but only exited the stairwell at 31 and 28. Why just those two floors? Remember, we're assuming Stemple is telling the truth–that the murderer rushed in, shot Madison Francis three times, then ran out, leaving the empty gun and dropping his mask. Then there's the gun."

"What about the gun?" asked Norm.

"Why did it run out of bullets? Nate's information was that it had a 25-shot magazine. Counting the shots on the 31st floor and the three that went into Madison Francis in Stemple's office, I only get to 17. Where are the other eight bullets?"

"Could he have used them to practice, or maybe he only had 17?" asked Norm.

"Maybe, but everything points to this being a very well thought out crime. How do you get a gun through security? The tampering with the door locks had to be planned well ahead of time. The murderer would also have to know exactly where Fisher's office was and that he would be in. With all that attention to detail, do you think he would leave eight bullets out?"

"What else?" asked Norm.

"Okay, why kill Stemple's assistant? Multiple shots–one to the head, one to the heart–when he only wounded Kirsten Grant with a single shot? Then leave Stemple alive with the gun? It doesn't make sense. Stemple says the gun was leveled at him, not Madison, then was switched to her for the first two shots."

"All those things make sense if Stemple did the shooting," said Norm.

"Then why phone 911 and wait for the police, still holding the gun and the mask? He must have known that he was dressed similarly to the murderer."

"He might have thought his story would fly," said Norm. "He probably didn't have time to get rid of the gun and his clothes."

"He had all the time he needed to do that before he phoned 911, but that's not part of the equation. We presume he's innocent, that someone set him up."

Dumping our plates and cups in the correct receptacles, Norm and I left the cafeteria and went back to our respective offices, Norm to work on alibis and finding the plaintiffs on Lester Fisher's current suits, and me to check on housing for the returning team. It was a school rule that freshmen roomed with freshmen, but Tip wanted Booker Oowaite to room with Avery Pierson, who was our senior center.

I was sitting back, contemplating how I would solve the housing issue, when my cell phone chimed. The screen said, "Janet Dorrinson."

"Hello, Rob," she began. I felt a cold sweat down my back and sides. Not a good-smelling, athletic sweat, but a foul-smelling one like the kind you got during final exams. Mrs. Dorrinson had called me twice in the last two years, and both times it was about someone who had been murdered–first her husband and then the principal of her husband's foundation. I waited for the shoe to drop.

"Hello, Mrs. Dorrinson," I said, trying to hide my unease.

"Are you getting nervous? And I thought we agreed that you would call me Janet."

"Nervous?" I wondered what my tell was that she could sense over the phone.

"Yes," said Janet. "The wedding is getting close."

The wedding. I took a deep breath. "I'm so lucky. Michelle and her bridesmaid, Leilah Watson, are doing all the work. I'm nervous about getting married, but not about the wedding. Well, a little about my speech."

"Rob, you don't have to give a speech. That's your Best Man's responsibility." Janet let out a small giggle.

"Good to know. One less thing I have to sweat. What can I do for you?" I asked.

"I was hoping you could help me with something. Jonathan had two cars. The Mercedes was totaled in the crash, as you know. His other car was his pet, his pride and joy. He bought it with the money from the sale of his first company. We used it to go on our honeymoon. It's been sitting in the garage unused for the last two years. I'd like you to have it."

I tried to remember what Nate had said about Dorrinson's cars. I could only remember that he had no tickets except one for failing to curb his wheels on Bush Street in San Francisco. It was one of the things that made his car accident so improbable. I couldn't remember his other car. I had certainly never seen it.

"I appreciate the offer," I said. "But I don't have a place to put it."

"Rob, I can't bear to sell it. It's a special car. I can't drive it. The clutch is too stiff. I think you would like it. Consider it a wedding gift. I've talked to Michelle. She thinks it would suit you. She even talked to a Mrs. O'Reilly, a neighbor two doors down from you. She has a double car garage and only one car. She told Michelle that you could rent the other side. She would appreciate the extra income as well."

It was just another instance in which women were two steps ahead of men. "What kind of car is it?" I asked, hoping that it didn't sound like my acceptance depended on the type of car being offered.

"It's a 2002 Dodge Viper convertible," said Janet. "It has 18,000 miles on it. We only used it on weekends, or to drive to Pebble Beach."

I drive a Camry Hybrid, but that is out of necessity. I couldn't afford better with the house payments taking most of my salary. I might drive a Camry, but I'm a Corvette type of guy. The Viper was a Corvette on steroids. It had a V10 engine and was built for pure speed. Vipers were also worth a bunch of money.

"That's an expensive car," I said. "I couldn't accept it."

"Yes, you could. You'd be doing me a great favor. I know that Jonathan would approve as well."

"Let me talk to Michelle," I said, already wondering what color it was. "And, again, thank you for the offer." I knew that since Janet had already talked with Michelle, I didn't really have a say in the matter. Driving away from the wedding in a Viper, we'd certainly fit in better at the Meadow Club than if we used the Camry for our get away. I shut off my cell phone, wondering how much insurance would run on a 2002 Dodge Viper. I never felt embarrassed driving my Camry. Well, maybe a little bit when both front doors were dented and I couldn't lower the windows. But just then, the memory of parking my Camry under Chase Center next to the rides of the Warrior players flashed through my mind–how absurd it had been. A Viper would have fit just fine.

CHAPTER 9

I looked at the time. It was only 12:45. I phoned Michelle. She was in her new office on 2nd Street. "I just got a call from Janet Dorrinson," I said when she picked up.

"I hope you graciously accepted the offer of the car?"

"Honey, it's a Dodge Viper. It's a classic. They don't make them anymore. It's worth a lot of money. I feel uncomfortable accepting it."

"From what I understand, you'd be doing her a favor. She has so many memories of her husband attached to it that she can't bring herself to sell it, and she's reminded of him every time she sees it in the garage."

"Still." I started to say something about it feeling like charity. I didn't get a chance.

"Tell you what. We're almost through setting up the office. I've pushed the staff pretty hard. Why don't I give them the rest of the day off, and you and I can go down to Woodside? I've got a lot of invoices to give Janet and a bunch of questions that I'd rather ask her in person. You can take a look at the car. If it needs a lot of work or you don't like it, you can politely refuse."

There it was. I was sure the trip to Woodside had already been planned by the women, just the deal about Mrs. O'Reilly's garage had been planned.

"I'll drive. I'll call you as soon as I get to the school," said Michelle, and she hung up, leaving no room to object.

—

Michelle's Prius's little four-cylinder engine hummed as soon as we passed San Francisco State University and started south on 280. Michelle kept it to 70 MPH and was constantly being passed. She'd phoned Janet Dorrinson and Janet was expecting us. It was the first time Michelle would be going to the house, so I gave her directions. When we got to the Dorrinson home, Janet had seen us turn into the driveway and was waiting for us on the top landing.

"Nice to see you both," she said as she ushered us inside. "Rob, Michelle and I have some Foundation business to discuss. I've ordered lunch from the Country Store. Would you mind picking it up?"

"Not at all," I said, extending my hand for Michelle's keys that were already in her purse.

"Here are the keys to Jonathan's car," said Janet. "Why don't you take it?" She pushed a button on the wall next to the door to the garage. "You can see how it drives and if you like it."

I saw Michelle's face turn serious as I took the keys. She could tell I was not pleased.

It was obviously a set-up, but I couldn't see any gracious way out of it. I took the door to the garage. Directly in front of me was Janet's Lexus SC. Then there was a space which I assumed had been for the Mercedes that Jonathan had been killed in. In the far space, bathed in sunlight from the open garage door, was a yellow Dodge Viper. I knew the Viper was almost 23 years old, but it looked brand new. It was gorgeous. The interior was done in brown leather with a slight reddish tint. I walked around it. Its design matched perfectly with what the car was, a high-powered beast.

I opened the door and slid behind the wheel. It had a push button start on the dashboard that I was sure wasn't original equipment. I touched it and the engine roared to life. The sound inside the garage reverberated in a low throaty throb. I let it warm up for a minute before putting it in gear. I was glad that whoever had parked it last had backed in. As Janet had said, the clutch was stiff, and I jerked a little until I got a feel for its release point. I left the driveway, passing around Michelle's Prius a little too fast. By the time I reached the Country Store, I was getting used to the car. I looked for a parking space that would be safe from door dings and shopping carts and went in to pick up the lunch that Janet had ordered.

I pulled out of the Country Store parking lot slowly, resisting the urge to take the car onto the 280. I looked at the gas gauge. The tank was full. I wondered if Janet had had someone prep it before I drove down with Michelle. Of course she had. This was part of a plan and it had worked. I was already in love with the car.

The women were waiting for their lunches, whatever business they had about the Foundation seemingly completed.

"How did you like the car?" asked Janet, as she put the sandwiches on plates that had been set on the breakfast room table. She tried to sound casual, but the effect was ruined by Michelle's chuckle.

"It's wonderful," I said. "It runs like it's brand new."

"Jonathan had a mechanic you can use for maintenance. All he really did was have it repainted yellow about ten years ago, and he replaced the original seats with new leather ones after I complained about the originals being too hard."

We had lunch. Janet had ordered me a salami and Swiss cheese on a hard roll, my go-to sandwich.

"Since Michelle drove you down, why don't you drive the car home and try it for a few weeks?" suggested Janet as she cleared the plates.

"Convenient," I said. "How long have you two been planning this?"

"Just a few days," said Janet. "But I started thinking about it when I heard that the junkyard man had replaced your doors."

"Seriously," I said. "I don't think we could afford the upkeep, and I'd feel terrible if anything happened to the car."

"Since Michelle now works for the Dorrinson Foundation, I thought we might run the title through it. That way the Foundation takes care of all that. And that will save a bunch of money in sales tax, plus I can use it as a tax write-off."

"I'm at a loss for words." I said, really meaning it.

"Good, then it's done," said Janet. "You've done me a great favor. I know Jonathan is smiling as well."

We said our good-byes and I climbed into the bright yellow Viper. I estimated my odds of getting a ticket on the way home at fifty-fifty. The car looked like it was speeding when it was parked.

I decided to stop by school. I told myself it was to pick up my laptop, but I knew in my heart that it was to show off the Viper. It was nearing 3:30 when I pulled in. I was disappointed that nobody saw me, despite revving the engine several times before I entered the underground garage, where I couldn't help doing it again just to hear the echo.

As I walked down the hallway, Norm came shooting out of his open office.

"Where have you been? I checked that your car's still in the lot, but I haven't been able to find you."

"It's a long story. I'll tell you when we're through. What's up?"

"Whistel came through with a bunch of current cases that Lester Fisher was working on. There might be more, but he came up with eight."

"Any possibles?"

"Yeah, a few. I haven't checked them out fully yet, but yeah. Two of the eight I've discounted. They weren't really suits. He just warned them that he would turn them in to the housing authority for making unauthorized improvements on properties they'd just bought. It looks like he was just shooting for a fee to keep quiet. He'd get zilch by turning them in, except for the Whistelblower reward. It seems like legalized blackmail to me. Fisher had a real knack for pissing people off."

"And the other six?"

"Five who fit the description, and three of those have offices in the same building as Fisher's firm."

"560 Mission. That's interesting."

"Yeah. I haven't had time to check alibis yet, or even read the full documents," said Norm. "I wanted to talk to you first about Franklin Whistel. He's getting nervous passing us information. He thinks the firm suspects a leak. We might not get anything more from him unless Nate increases his Christmas gift."

"More likely Nate would threaten to tell Whistel's partners if he didn't keep feeding us. Have you spoken to your dad?"

"Nope, the less I do that the better."

"Okay, I'll talk to Nate about Whistel. You keep working on the new leads and those that are still active on the old list. Now, come with me and I'll show you what I've been doing."

Even in the garage lighting, the Viper seemed to glow.

"Oh, wow!" said Norm, walking around the car. "Where did you get this?"

"A gift from one of my previous clients. Not a job that I did for Nate, by the way."

"Some gift."

I went back in, leaving Norm circling the car, and picked up my laptop. Norm was gone when I got back. I threw my laptop case onto the passenger's seat and took off across the city and the Golden Gate Bridge in my new ride. Our get-away car when leaving the Meadow Club after the wedding had just been upgraded.

Michelle heard me coming up the street and greeted me with the garage door opener to Mrs. O'Reilly's house. More proof that I hadn't stood a chance. Not that it mattered. The Viper and I were already one.

We had to get permission from Mrs. O'Reilly to move some boxes. The Viper was wider than whatever other vehicle had occupied the space. That done, we parked and walked the sixty feet to our house.

"How did this come up?" I asked as we opened our front door.

"Janet came to look at the new space three days ago and told me she was upset about selling the car. She asked if it was something you would like."

"And you said yes without asking me?"

"It was more, 'Why don't I bring him down to look at it?' than yes."

We went in. She could tell I was mad. I wondered what it was that was upsetting me. I liked the car, and giving it to me had obviously made Janet Dorrinson happy. I finally realized that it was the fact that the decision had basically been taken from me and it seemed like charity. Without much being said, I ordered a pizza, then went in and took a long shower.

When I got out of the bathroom and dressed, the pizza had arrived. We ate in silence. I decided to clean up and then go to my office to review my notes on the Lester Fisher case. I knew I was being small, but I was still pissed.

When it was time to go to bed, I brushed my teeth before Michelle used the bathroom. I was under the covers when Michelle came in and slipped into bed.

After a minute she said, "My mom has been giving me advice since I first told her I loved you. Most of it is just mothers' stuff, but she did tell me something that I feel is important. She said never to go to bed mad."

She leaned over and kissed me. I felt tears dropping on my cheeks.

"I'm sorry I didn't tell you about the car as soon as Janet mentioned it. I'll try never to make a decision about our life without you again."

I could tell my anger was still trying to control me, but my love for Michelle was pushing it out, like fog on a summer day.

"I'm not sure what upset me," I said, returning her kiss. "Part of it was that it was done behind my back. Part of it is that it seems like charity. Ever since I was little, I've loved giving gifts more than receiving them. I think it could have been because my parents weren't well off until I was almost out of college. I've often felt poor and hated getting anything I didn't work for. I love the car. It's an extravagance that I probably never would have bought myself. I probably would have said no if you had told me beforehand, if only because of its worth. It's over, though. It's done. Let's not talk about it anymore." We hugged, then assumed the spoon position. It brought feelings that pushed out whatever anger was remaining. It was a while before either of us fell asleep, but when we did, we weren't mad.

CHAPTER 10

Since I had driven the Viper home, I had to pick up my Camry, which was still at school. Michelle gave me a ride in the next morning. I hoped to get a full day's work done without being pulled in three different directions. As I sat down at my desk and unpacked my laptop, my plan started to fall apart. I remembered that I hadn't called Nate about Whistel and to relate what Norm had found out about the additional lawsuits.

It was late enough in the morning that Nate would be at his office and would have already relieved himself of the two cups of coffee he habitually drank on the way in. I was right on both counts.

"What do you have for me?" demanded Nate.

It took a while to outline what Norm had discovered about Fisher's current lawsuits. Nate was particularly interested in the three men with offices in the same building.

"Check those guys out carefully," said Nate. "What about Stemple's list of people who might hold a grudge against him?"

"I haven't gotten it yet. I'll drop by the jail this afternoon and see if he's finished it."

"I'm going to get my expert to examine the mask that was dropped," said Nate.

I'd forgotten about the mask, other than to wonder why the murderer had taken it off before he entered the fire stairwell. "How long will that take?"

"It depends on the DA. She can't hold on to it forever. Later." The usual Nate farewell.

I'd just started going over our schedule for the upcoming season. We wouldn't have to finalize it for another two weeks, but it was pretty well set. We'd taken a page from the Gonzaga playbook and booked our pre-conference games with the highest ranked squads we could. We had also used some of the half-million gift from our anonymous donor to pay teams to play us on our home court. Some, like Indiana, we booked into Chase Center, figuring our home court of 4500 seats would sell out because of our ranking and Indiana's national reputation in basketball. It somewhat reduced our chance of a victory, but it made us a lot more money in tickets as well as raised our national profile.

We had one more spot that we could fill before this year's Christmas tournament in Maui. I was looking at possible opponents when my desk phone rang.

"Coach," said Winfred Ramsey.

A call from compliance was never a good thing. It was usually about one of our kids failing a random drug test, or someone not completing a course that put him below the required number of units. The possibilities were endless, and most of them weren't good. I sat up straight, expecting the worst.

"Good news, Coach. The NCAA just called and Simu Vuksan has been cleared as an amateur. You can go ahead and sign him."

"I thought you said they would definitely not review his file for another two months?"

"That's what I was told. It's very unusual, but good for us."

Compliance was our program's watchdog, sheriff, and hangman. What was unusual was that Ramsey had said "good news."

"Win, I want to be absolutely clear about this. Could you recheck Simu's eligibility status with the NCAA and also his TOEFL score? I don't want any questions raised when I bring this to Tip."

"I can do that," said Win. "Do you suspect some irregularity?"

"No. It's just that I'm not used to things falling into place so easily."

D'Jarl must have been listening. He entered just as I hung up and sat down across from me.

"When did the NCAA ever do anybody any favors?" I said, as he shifted his weight.

"Hmm," said D'Jarl, under his breath. He looked away from me, then broke into a grin. "Did you by chance mention this to my father-in-law?"

I racked my brain. "I might have in passing," I said. "He needed two additional invitations to the wedding for his security detail. I could have mentioned Simu then. Why?"

"He called me a day ago and wanted to know what the problem was with Simu's eligibility. I gave him the details. It was just after Simu passed the TOEFL."

"You don't think he pressured the NCAA, do you?"

"I don't know that he would pressure them, but I'm sure he has a friend or two in the organization at a pretty high level."

"Damn," I said.

"If Ramsey finds we're clear, I'd bring it to Tip and get the kid signed immediately." D'Jarl reached across the desk and gave me a high five.

I had an uneasy feeling. Things were going too well. It always seemed that way before a disaster struck.

—

An hour later Win Ramsey called, just as I was getting up from my desk.

"Everything checks out," said Win.

Probably with one of the bigwigs suggesting they look at it sooner, I thought. Thank you, Mr. Matobi.

Tip grinned when I told him I'd asked compliance to check a second time on Simu Vuksan's eligibility. "I'll phone Vuksan right now," said Tip, looking at the wall clock and adding the nine hours that Serbia was ahead of us. It would be just before 9 pm.

My conversation with Vuksan's parents was short and sweet. The father's English was better than Simu's. The parents were happy, Tip was happy, Simu was being cool, but I could tell he was excited. Tip explained that he would send the scholarship offer and the National Letter of Intent, and that they had to be signed and sent back directly to Admissions. It was a good conversation, one I always enjoyed being part of, regardless of whether it was on the phone or in person. For an 18-year-old, it was a life-changing event.

Coach Jovanovic phoned fifteen minutes after I'd left Tip.

"Coach MacKee!" came the now familiar greeting. "Good news, ech? Simu's parents are very happy. Can't wait to come San Francisco."

"We're glad everything worked out as well. Simu will fit in nicely this year, and next year he'll be ready to be the team's leader. We just signed another recruit as Simu's classmate. He has a chance to be as good as Bogdan in a couple of years. They'll make a good pair."

"Good to hear. Good to hear."

D'Jarl came in, and I put the phone on speaker. Jovanovic wanted to know about Booker Oowaite, the recruit I'd mentioned who would be Simu's classmate.

"Goot, goot," said Jovanovic when D'Jarl had finished telling him about the big Native American from Oklahoma. "Simu not have good big man since Bogdan left. You have to teach Simu how to use him."

We said our goodbyes and hung up.

"This is going to be a fun year," said D'Jarl, offering me another high five.

Exciting, at least, I thought, as D'Jarl went back to his own office. I hoped that Simu wouldn't come to San Francisco on the day of our wedding.

I was starting to get hungry. I wasn't sure if it was because it was time to eat or because my morning activities and phone calls had burnt up a mess of calories. I looked at my phone. It was half past two. No wonder I was hungry.

I was standing up, checking my back pocket for my wallet, when Norm Hart came in. He flopped down in my spare chair. I could tell something was wrong.

"My car was broken into," said Norm. "They broke the driver side window and popped the glove box and the trunk."

"Where were you parked?" I asked.

"On Mission. I was checking the alibis of the three guys who work at 560 and are being sued by Fisher. I wasn't through, but the parking meter was about to expire on my car. I left the building, fed the meter another six dollars in quarters, and went back to the building. When I returned to the car, the window was broken, the glove box was open, and my stuff was gone from the trunk."

"That's not unusual," I said. "If I believe the papers, there were something like 15,000 car break-ins last year. Did you leave anything in the car?"

"Nothing in the car, but the trunk had some important stuff."

"Like what?" I asked.

"For one thing, the files I'd been working on for you and Nate," said Norm, "and my computer and my hand gun."

"Your gun?"

"Yeah. A Colt Mustang, semi-automatic, and its holster."

"I didn't know you carried a gun."

"Dad insisted on it years ago when I graduated from law school and started helping him with some of his criminal cases. It's registered. I didn't bring it to Europe with me. It's strange that whoever did this didn't take a present that I'd bought for mom. It was wrapped and sitting on top of the files."

"Have you reported this to the police?" I asked.

"First thing I did after I told my dad. They were more interested in the gun than in the fact that my car was broken into."

"Why would the thief take the paper files and leave a wrapped present? It's not like they're worth anything. Can you reconstruct them?"

"No problem," said Norm, sitting up a little straighter. "I record the interviews on my phone, then transfer the info and data to the files in a backup hard drive. It will be a pain in the ass but I can do it. You don't happen to know any glass guys, do you?"

"I know one if you don't mind driving to Palo Alto." I scanned my contacts and pressed Burt Fulbert.

"Excelsior Auto Salvage."

"Hi, Burt. This is Rob MacKay. I was wondering if you had a driver's side window for a…" I looked at Norm.

"2015 BMW 5 series sedan," Norm said quickly.

I repeated this to Burt.

"I can have one here by tomorrow morning. That do?"

I turned to Norm, who nodded.

"Great. My friend's name is Norm Hart. He's working with me on a case."

"I'll take care of him, boss." I could hear Burt spit as he hung up.

I wrote down Burt's address and gave it to Norm. I was still wondering why only Norm's files, computer, and gun were taken. Couldn't the thief carry any more? A present didn't seem like too much to pack.

"How big was the gift for your mother?" I asked.

"Not big. It was just a bracelet."

Another mystery. As if we didn't have enough already.

CHAPTER 11

Buddy Doyle sat at a corner table in a small restaurant and coffee shop on 2nd Street between Mission and Market. The sign above its entrance proudly proclaimed FOOD - COFFEE. It was the kind of place you would never think to enter, but it always seemed to be full. He was waiting for Buzz, a boyhood friend from the teenaged "No Name Gang" that roamed South of Market some twenty years earlier. Both he and Buzz had moved on–Doyle to a life of petty crime and Buzz to who knew what. What Buddy did know is that Buzz occasionally called him to do a job, and he paid well. From what he surmised from the work, Buzz had moved up in the world and was successful, if not rich. On the table in front of Buddy was a brown paper shopping bag with a loaf of French bread sticking out of the top.

Buzz had called him and given him a description of a guy who was inside the 560 Mission building. He wanted the guy followed, wanted to know who he was and where he lived.

Buddy only knew Buzz by that name, and as far as Buzz knew, he was just Buddy. It was a separation they were careful to maintain.

Buzz arrived and saw Buddy. He was dressed in slacks and a white button-down shirt. His shoes were black and shiny, another indication that he had turned respectable. Buddy wondered if he should ask for more money when he took these jobs.

"I followed him when he left the building," said Buddy as Buzz sat down. "Your description was perfect. He went to his car and fed the meter, opened the trunk, left some of the files he was carrying, then went back to the building carrying his briefcase. I didn't know how long he might be in there, so I opened the car and got the guy's papers, then popped the trunk. A pistol was lying next to the files and the computer." Buddy indicated the shopping bag between them.

"You're sure nobody followed you?"

Buddy looked at Buzz with raised eyebrows. "How long have you known me?"

Buddy nudged the shopping bag toward Buzz. It was heavier than Buzz would have expected. There was a laptop computer, three manila files, a gun, and two pieces of loose paper that were the car's registration and insurance. Buzz took out the car's registration and saw that the address was a P.O. box.

"Do you want the gun?" asked Buddy.

"Better you keep it for a while," said Buzz. "If I need it, I'll let you know. How was it you got it and the files?"

"Like I said, I saw him put them in the trunk. I thought it would be good to take more than just the registration, so I popped the trunk and there they were. Same with the computer and the gun."

"You can have the computer back after I look at it," said Buzz, slipping Buddy five crisp hundreds.

"Thanks for the Cs." Buddy pocketed the pistol and started to get up to leave. Buzz put his hand out and pulled him back down.

"I leave first," said Buzz. "Wait five minutes. Then you can go."

Buddy suspected that this was because Buzz didn't want himself followed. The guy was creepy, but he was always good for a quick pay-off, and five hundred, a gun, and a computer were not bad for fifteen minutes' work. Buddy watched Buzz leave the coffee shop and turn left. He was carrying the shopping bag. The French bread was purely camouflage, and it was stale.

I was getting to be a regular at the San Francisco jail. The sheriff nodded at me, calling me MacKay. He not only knew my name, but he seemed to know who I was there to see. Fifteen minutes later I was in the room with Stewart Stemple. Every time I saw him, he was a little less cocky. Jail was taking its toll.

"Do you have the list I asked you to prepare?" I asked, seeing the yellow pad in his hand.

"Yeah," he answered, tearing a sheet off the top. He handed it to me.

I looked at the paper. It was a list of about fifteen names.

"What is this?" I asked, looking up from the list.

"It's a list of people who would wish me dirt."

"But it's just the names, no reason, no hint of why, or of who they are. Do you expect me to guess why they're mad at you?"

"You didn't say you wanted all that," said Stemple.

"I've spent the last two days checking people's whereabouts, checking alibis. Then you give me this and expect me to figure out why they hate your guts." I threw the list back across the table. "Take it back and put down as much information as you can about each one. Be specific about what their grudges with you are. Give me something to work with."

"Look, I'm the one in jail for something I didn't do."

"Yes, and you'll stay there unless Nate can pin it on someone else, or at least put doubt in the minds of the jury." I realized I was being hard on him. But I was stretched thin, and having Stemple waste my time got to me. As far as I was concerned, the visit was over.

"Listen. I'm a fixer," said Stemple. "Officially I'm a financial advisor and real estate investor. I do those things, but I make a lot of money because people hire me to get things done in San Francisco. I know people. I know the system. When I'm successful, it's like being a lawyer. Someone wins, someone loses. Someone's happy, someone's pissed that I got involved. Some of what you want me to put down in writing will affect powerful people who may have done something slightly illegal."

"I see. I'll still need the information if you're going to get cleared. I'll run it by Nate before I get anybody upset. Put down the information in as much detail as possible, and I'll be back tomorrow to pick it up."

I got up and rang the bell to be let out. I had to remind myself to keep the mindset that Stemple was innocent.

A fixer. I had several other names for it.

I never tire of driving across the Golden Gate Bridge. My grandmother had been let out of junior high school on the bridge's opening day and had joined most of San Francisco in walking across the span on May 27, 1937; no cars until the following day. My father told me about driving across the bridge with his dad when he was 12 on the day the construction loan was paid off. He'd asked his dad if now the twenty-five cent toll would be removed, and his dad had laughed. Just like my dad to think of the economic implications. The toll was now eight dollars and going up next year. Maybe it was a good thing that Dad had moved out of state. Looking at the view–the red-leaded towers, the hills of Marin–almost made the cost worthwhile.

I was just entering the Robin Williams rainbow tunnel when my cell phone rang. It was Norm. I answered it and immediately lost the connection. Once I was out of the tunnel, and again had service, I called Norm back.

"I just found something else that was taken," said Norm.

"I'm driving. I might lose you again. If I do, I'll call you when I get home. What else is missing?"

"The registration and insurance information from the glove box."

"What?"

"I went looking for the insurance so I could give it to your guy, Burt, tomorrow," said Norm. "I know it was there because I'd just replaced the proof of insurance slip when I got back to town and took the car out of storage."

"Anything else?"

"No. Just the gun, the files, and my computer."

I thought for a minute as I reached the flats of Sausalito, the wildly painted houseboats on my right with Marin City on my left. "That settles it. This was no ordinary car break in. No snatch and grab. That they left a wrapped package should have been enough, but taking the car's information makes no sense unless you were targeted."

"Yeah, that's what Nate thinks as well. He says I probably stirred something up by asking questions. Because they took the files, he thinks it involves the case we're working on."

"Why the insurance papers?" I asked.

"My name and address," said Norm. "But the registration and insurance only have Nate's post office box. So they won't know my address."

"Nate insisted I do the same when I started working for him," I said. "He said it was best to keep personal information hidden when you worked for a criminal attorney. Now I see why. Does your dad feel you're in danger? Does he want you to stop?"

"Hell no," said Norm. "He says I must be ruffling some feathers. He did say to be careful, that if Stemple is innocent, the real murderer is still out there. He's getting me a replacement gun."

"Tomorrow Stemple is writing up a list of people who have it in for him."

"I thought you were getting that today?" asked Norm.

"I did too. He gave me a list of names with no explanation as to why they would be mad at him. I threw it back at him. He said he was reluctant to put down the reasons because a lot of important people might get upset."

"Oh boy! Doesn't he understand that he's being charged with a double murder?"

"I think it's beginning to sink in," I said as I pulled into my driveway. "Jail has a way of emphasizing that point. I'm going to pick up the revised list tomorrow around noon. Would you like to meet for lunch at Mel's? We can see what he's so worried about."

"Sounds good. Mel's on Geary at one," said Norm, and we hung up.

I had an hour before Michelle would be home, so I got out a few tools and started to work on the bedroom blinds that let in the morning sun. I couldn't figure out a way to have them close any more tightly than they did. Then I remembered seeing a thin strip of felt weather stripping at Home Depot. I thought it might work.

I jumped in my Camry; no Dodge Viper of mine would ever grace the parking lot of Home Depot. I was back in less than half an hour. The color of the stripping almost matched the paint on the shutters, not that it would ever show. I temporarily tacked a length on the edge of a slat that faced the window. Bingo. When I closed the slats, no light entered on that row. It took very little time to cut and glue the rest of the stripping into place. I had one window done when Michelle arrived. I felt that I had at least accomplished one thing that day. I showed Michelle. I think she was impressed. Not only did no light enter when the slats were closed, but the clack that had accompanied their use was now gone. I still had two other windows to do, but it would require another trip to Home Depot.

Michelle ordered pizza–our usual, anchovies on my half.

"You remember that Saturday is my wedding shower?" said Michelle as we finished our last slice.

"Of course." In fact, it had slipped my mind. The shower was one of three that were going to be held over the next month. This one was for all the friends that the wedding mothers still had in the area, women who had seen both of us grow up. There were a dozen of them, too many for our small front room. Janet Dorrinson had offered her house in Woodside, and it was readily accepted by Michelle and the two mothers-in-law to be. I had no responsibilities other than to make sure my office was converted into a second guest bedroom and was ready for my mom and dad. That, and to entertain my and Michelle's dads while the women partied.

CHAPTER 12

Stemple entered the interview room and tossed his list to me. He was not happy. I recognized many of the names, most of them actually. On it were politicians, the city's wealthy, and many of the new elite of the tech industry. The details that he provided on their dealings were even more damaging than their names. I didn't want to go over them with him at this time. I wanted to read them in full and determine how they might figure into the case, if at all. Then I'd talk with Nate about how to proceed.

"I've done what you wanted," said Stemple. "Now get me out of here."

"I'll ask Nate what he can do," I said, thinking that Stemple was likely to be behind bars for a long time. After seeing the list, Nate would have plenty of people to pick from who would like to see Stewart Stemple come to harm. They also might want him free to stop the information from becoming public. I just didn't see how any of it was going to overcome the strong evidence against the man.

I met Norm at Mel's as planned. He'd been out of touch with what was happening in the City for at least two years, but he still remembered many of the names on Stemple's list.

I ordered the Mel's burger, Norm got the pancakes and sausage. I suspected that Norm's day started a lot later than mine as a rule and that he hadn't had time for breakfast before driving to Palo Alto with a broken driver's side window.

While we ate, we went over the list Stemple had provided. There were fourteen names.

"Whoa!" said Norm as he glanced at the list. "I knew this was how things were done in the City, but having it put down on paper... wow."

"The double murder charge must be sinking in," I said. "We should check physical appearances, but I doubt many of these people would dirty their own hands."

We went over each of the names, noting the seriousness of the service Stemple had provided.

"Would you come with me when I give this to Nate?" I asked.

"I'd prefer not to. I don't mind working for him, but I'd rather not work with him. We always seem to get into an argument about my career choices."

"I'll be there to keep things on track. It would be good for both of us to hear what Nate wants to do with this list. It would save time and avoid confusion."

"Yeah. I see that. Okay, when do you want to see him?"

"I'll see if he's free after the team practices, say three-thirty today?" I took my phone out, speed-dialed Nate's cell, and made the appointment. I was not going to give Norm time to back out.

"Your friend Burt is a trip," said Norm as I hung up. "He pulled the door panel and replaced the window in under an hour. I don't know what you did for him, but he didn't want to charge me. I slipped him three hundred anyway. It's less than my deductible and it doesn't go on his books. Window works great."

—

Nate seemed happy to see us. He actually stood and shook my hand and did the same with Norm. I couldn't help but wonder, seeing them together, if Norm would go bald and put on weight as he got older. He and Nate were the same height, but Norm's facial features were much finer. As pleased as Nate was to see us, Norm looked just as uncomfortable. We sat down in front of his desk and were offered coffee, a first for me in Nate's office.

"You should know about this," said Nate, holding up a sheet of paper, then handing it to Norm. "The District Attorney's office is charging you for leaving an unsecured gun in your car."

"What!" said Norm, almost rising from his chair. "The car was broken into. The gun was locked in the trunk."

"I know," said Nate. "She's just covering her ass in case the gun is used later. That, and she doesn't like me. It's nothing to worry about. I hope you took pictures of the broken window and the open glove compartment."

"Yeah," said Norm. "So did Rob's friend who fixed the window."

"Like I said, it's not a problem," said Nate. "You two must be stirring up some real dirt if someone breaks into your car for your registration, insurance, and some files."

"That's what we thought," I said, hoping to give Norm a chance to cool down. "The files that were taken had nothing that can't be reconstructed."

"It actually gives me something to use in court," said Nate. "Who would do that if not to stop our investigation? So why did you want to meet, if it wasn't about the break-in?"

"I got a list from Stemple of people he'd screwed. At first he just gave me a list of names. That was yesterday."

"So he was more forthcoming today?"

"You could say that," I said, handing Nate the legal pad that Stemple had used to list the fourteen names and the reasons why these people had a problem with him.

Nate read the first couple of accounts, then quickly flicked through the remaining pages, taking in the names and scanning the offenses. "Damn," he said. "If I'd known he had this, I'd have represented him pro bono. This is worth its weight in gold. I could retire three times over with this."

"Norm and I wanted some direction before we started digging into it," I said.

"Dig into it! You'll do nothing of the kind. Whatever you do, tread lightly. Find out if any of these people fit the description of the gunman. Check their whereabouts, but don't do anything with the information Stemple put down. Not yet, at least."

"If we don't use the list to clear Stemple, what will you do with it?" asked Norm.

"You know how many favors I can call in with this list? It'll make me practically bulletproof in this town."

"What about Stemple?" asked Norm, voicing my own question.

"I might use one name to argue reasonable doubt. I only need one. That's why the profile and the alibi are important. The rest I'll bank."

"We'll need a copy of those," I said.

"Of course," said Nate.

I expected him to buzz his assistant and give her the pages to copy, but Nate got up and left Norm and me sitting alone sipping coffee. He returned five minutes later with two sets of copies. The details had been covered after each name. It was basically the same list that I'd tossed back at Stemple. I was surprised. Norm just let out a chuckle. We got up to leave. Nate stood as well and walked around the desk.

"Great work," he said. "You've got a real knack." He clapped Norm on the back. Norm was his son. I now understood why I'd been offered coffee.

"Now you see why I don't want to be a lawyer?" said Norm, as we rode the elevator down to the parking garage.

"You don't have to practice criminal law. There are hundreds of other types of law to practice."

"Not in this town. Not for me. I would always be Nate's son."

"He seems genuinely happy that you're helping with this case."

"Yeah. We actually get along quite well when he's not trying to get me to practice with him." Norm looked relieved when we reached the car and started driving back to the school.

"How do you want to do this?" I asked. "I was thinking we should start with the physical descriptions, then look at the ones who fit to see what Stemple did to them and if it involved Fisher."

"How can you do that? I saw the copies he made," said Norm.

"Oh, I forgot to tell Nate. I made full copies at school before we went downtown."

Norm let out a belly laugh and hit me on the shoulder. It was a grammar school punch thrown by a grown man and my shoulder hurt. It was worth it to see Norm happy.

Half an hour after we arrived at school, Norm had separated the names on the list by whether they fit the murderer's physical appearance, and we started on the five who fit.

As it turned out, getting Fisher's appointment schedule wasn't a big problem. The calendars for the lawyers in Fisher's office were shared online. It was the best way to know exactly what each of the forty-seven attorneys was doing at any given time. Whistel was in no danger of further scrutiny by copying the last three months of Fisher's appointments and sending the information to me. I decided to check all fourteen names, not just the favored five. I wasn't as accomplished on the computer as Michelle, but I knew how to select FIND, so the search took less than an hour. Fisher had met with seven of the people on the list. Some multiple times. It was time to go home.

I was nearing my car in the parking lot when I heard the squeal of tires. A Beamer pulled up and stopped in back of my car. It was Tip. I took a deep breath and relaxed. Tip left the car running and got out.

"I'm glad I caught you, I didn't expect you to still be here."

I felt a surge of guilt letting Tip think that I was working on team stuff, but I kept my mouth shut. "What's up?" I asked.

"Daly from compliance called me on my cell. Simu Vuksan will be able to practice with the team prior to the start of the school year as long as it's in open gym, but he won't be able to travel with us on the European trip."

"Bummer," I said. "Still, it's a win that we know he's eligible to play, and we have the NIL money to support him."

"I guess I wanted it all," said Tip. "It would have been great to showcase two European star players during our trip. You can see how a relationship with a coach helped with Bogdan and Simu. You and I will be spending a lot of time developing relationships with the coaches on the national teams we play. It's important for the future of our program."

"It's too late to phone Serbia now," I said. "Do you want me with you in the morning when you call?"

"That's why I was coming to school. I couldn't remember when we last called them. We're only allowed one call a week, and I didn't want to blow this after everything has gone so well."

"I'd have to check his file," I said. "Calls to Coach Jovanovic don't count, and neither do the calls from them to us."

"You're going to be a fine head coach someday," said Tip, clapping me on the back. He got into his car and backed away, did a three-point turn, and left the garage.

How lucky was I to have Tip as a boss? The stress of working for Nate Hart and the fast-approaching wedding were forgotten in the warmth of his praise.

CHAPTER 13

"Remember the first shower is this Saturday," said Michelle as she placed a plate of eggs and bacon in front of me.

"Is there anything I can do?" I asked.

"Not a thing. Mom and Janet have done all the work. Your mom helped too. The shower is mainly for the friends they still have in the area, although Leilah will be there to take notes."

"When are your mother and father coming in?"

"Friday," said Michelle. "They and your parents are arriving at SFO at about the same time. Dad's renting a car and the four of them are driving here together. Would you make sure your desk is clean? That will be your parents' bedroom."

I knew I was getting off easy. The truth was, I had no idea what her shower entailed. I knew Michelle was having three of them and that she'd be receiving presents, but that was it.

"I'm taking the men to basketball practice on Saturday morning. Then we play at the Olympic Club in the afternoon. So the bathroom will be yours alone."

"The ladies are so looking forward to seeing Janet's home," said Michelle.

"What types of presents will you get?" I asked, knowing that my mom's friends would try to outdo each other.

"Stuff to set up our household," said Michelle. "I've signed up for a registry at several stores."

"I could use a saber saw." I saw nothing funny in my comment, but Michelle almost doubled over with laughter.

When she recovered her breath, she stood, bent over me, and kissed my forehead. She said, "I don't think the ladies know how handy you are around the house."

I could see that Michelle was thinking about our house and how full it would be over the weekend. She said, "I think it's sad that Janet has no children."

I had nothing to say to that. I cleaned the table and pans and left for school.

Tip beat me in, but not by much. His BMW was still ticking when I parked next to it and went directly to his office. D'Jarl was already there, having walked from his home. As soon as I sat, Tip grabbed his phone.

"Mr. Vuksan, good evening," said Tip.

"And good morning to you, Coach Pennington," came the reply.

The only difficult part of the conversation was when we learned that Simu would not be arriving in San Francisco until the day before the fall term started. He would stay in Belgrade and play basketball with his Serbian team through the summer. Both D'Jarl and I were surprised that Tip didn't try to talk Mr. Vuksan into sending his son earlier. The call ended with congratulations on both sides. Simu told us that Coach Jovanovic was going to bring him to Spain and Paris to watch us play.

"Simu," said Tip. "Would you ask Coach Jovanovic to send me any films he has on the teams we are going to play? The only footage we can find here is promotional stuff, not game film."

"I do right away," said Simu, and we ended the call.

"I thought you would try to get Simu here earlier to practice with the team," said D'Jarl as soon as Tip sat back in his chair.

"I wasn't going to change his mind," said Tip.

I left Tip's office and went to see if Norm was in. He wasn't. I thought I'd have less chance of being disturbed if I stayed in Norm's little office.

I started a spreadsheet with the names of the people we'd identified who could have it in for both Lester Fisher and Stewart Stemple. We'd gone through the names by hand earlier, but I thought it would be best to do a more thorough search.

I started with the people Fisher had sued, then added the names that had unresolved actions, finishing up with the names on Stemple's list. I was almost through when Norm came in at 11 am. He added a column for gun knowledge, one for physical appearance, and a third for office location. We were through with the spreadsheet by noon.

A quick lunch at the Arguello Market and we were back at school. I left Norm and checked the basketball offices. The game films hadn't come in yet.

We worked steadily for an hour and a half, coming up with four names that seemed most likely. All were men. All had a legal problem with Fisher, had access to the building, and were on Stemple's list.

"I'd like to add one more," said Norm. "He's got a solid alibi but checks all the other boxes." The list read:

George Krusen
James Tennet
Stanford Quoc

John Jensen

Lance LaBarr

I was looking at the five names when Norm got up and stood behind me, pointing down at the list.

"I've talked to everyone on that list except Jensen. All but Stanford Quoc have alibis," he said.

"Do you have any idea which one Nate will pick for his straw man?" I asked, wondering if Norm had better insight into his dad's intentions than I did.

"With the motives they all have, and the opportunity to know the building, I don't think he'll give a damn. Any one of them will do."

I was taken aback by Norm's comment. "We're supposed to be finding out who did it. That means one," I said. "Remember what Nate said. 'Assume that Stemple is innocent.'"

"Yeah, right. Stemple is dirty," said Norm. "You saw the dirty tricks he pulled for the guys on his list. You don't think he's capable of murder? The evidence is overwhelming."

"Still, I think we should be looking for the real killer. After all, someone on the outside broke into your car–for what, your registration and some files? I think your gun was just a perk."

I knew I was right. There was no way Stemple could have arranged the break-in, and more than that, he had no reason to do it. No, it was someone on our list, and probably someone Norm had already questioned. I had an increasing feeling that Stemple, as unsavory as he was, and as much as the evidence was stacked against him, might be telling the truth.

"We should take this to Nate," I said.

"Not before we get as much information on these guys as possible. He'll want that."

—

We took the next two hours with Google developing a profile for each of the five people on the list. It was time to go home when we finished. I was beat, but I went back to the basketball offices. Tip was just leaving.

"The game films came in. I had them put on your and D'Jarl's desks on flash drives. We don't have a lot of time to prepare for the three teams we'll be facing. Pay particular attention to the international rules we'll be playing under."

I could tell that Tip wasn't happy that I was not there when Jovanovic sent the films. I was secretly happy that D'Jarl was also absent. Best to share the blame. Regardless, my evening would be busy.

The first minute I spent looking at the film told me we had our hands full. The Spanish team was semi-pro and included many players who had played in the Olympics three years before. They were only missing a few players who had left to play in the NBA. They were big and fast and had a couple guards who could shoot the lights out from the 3-point line. Maybe Tip wasn't upset because D'Jarl and I weren't there. Maybe it was because he'd seen the film and was afraid that our players would be embarrassed, or worse, lose confidence. I called D'Jarl.

"D'Jarl, have you picked up the game films that came in?"

"No," was D'Jarl's reply.

"They came in late this afternoon. Tip put them on a drive and left them on our desks." I didn't want it to seem like I thought D'Jarl wasn't being responsible, so I added, "I stopped by Tip's office by chance and he told me about them. I just got home and looked at them. I thought I'd better call you right away. I've only looked at Spain, but they're scary."

"Thanks," said D'Jarl and hung up. I had no doubt that he was already out the door.

I'd finished with the Spanish clips and had started dissecting the French team. It was no better. If anything, they were bigger than the Spaniards. Their offensive movement and the ways they set screens for their shooters were complicated and well done. I went over the same play three times, seeing how they freed up their shooter. I paused the film. It made me think of the murders at 560 Mission. The murderer's movements were well planned and precise, if he had intended to escape leaving Stemple literally holding a smoking gun. Where did he go with only two doors allowing him entry back into the building from the fire stairwell? I made a mental note to look at the fire stairs again.

My cell phone rang.

"Damn," said D'Jarl, before I could get out a word. "The international game has gotten a lot better in the five years since I played. Shall we get to school a couple hours early tomorrow so we can give Tip a plan?"

"Sure, say 7:30."

Michelle got home just before I'd finished watching the French film. Our moods couldn't have been more different. She was exuberant. They had just finalized the first disbursement from the Dorrinson Foundation under Michelle's supervision. It was small, only a $50,000 grant to provide musical instruments for a charter school in San Leandro. The amount didn't matter; it had been her first disbursement, there had been no glitches, and the staff seemed happy with her as the boss. Halfway through her step-by-step recounting of the grant procedure, she stopped and asked, "What's wrong?"

"Nothing," I said, unable to hide what I was really feeling.

"Nothing?" Michelle was not going to let it end there.

"It's just that I've gone over the films of two of the teams we'll be playing on the trip and they're good, really good. They also gave me some new questions about the murders."

Michelle came up behind me and kissed my neck. The neck nuzzle was easy and unstrained. It felt good, and her confidence in me helped.

"I don't think our wings will be able to guard theirs one on one."

"You and Tip will figure it out," said Michelle. "You always do."

She wanted to celebrate her first disbursement. We went to Marin Joe's for dinner. It was just what I needed: a plate full of sweetbreads with ravioli on the side. It was either Michelle or the stomach full of sweetbreads, but I was much more relaxed when we got home. After some quick, celebratory love-making, I fell asleep.

CHAPTER 14

D'Jarl arrived at school at the same time I did. He drove, which was unusual, as it was sunny in San Francisco, even though the fog had been thick as I crossed the Golden Gate. He had a large smile on his face that lit up the dark garage. I was worried about what I'd seen on the game films, so seeing him smile as he got out of his car should have helped. It didn't.

"Why are you so worried?" he asked. I didn't remind him that the first thing he'd said the previous night after viewing the films was "Damn!"

"And you aren't?" We entered the offices and turned on the lights. It was cold. I got the space heaters out of Tip's office and brought them to D'Jarl's.

"Okay," I said. "What you got?"

"Defense is going to be tough. Tip will have some ideas on that, but I think I see something on offense, that is if our guards and wings can pick it up." He went over what he had planned, and we looked at the Spanish team film to see how it would work.

Tip came in at 8:30 and opened D'Jarl's door. He seemed surprised to see us. He looked at the space heaters I'd pilfered and nodded.

"You two seem busy," he said. "Internationals look good, huh?"

"D'Jarl's got some ideas on how we can score on the Spanish squad," I said.

For the next hour, we worked on our scheme with Tip leading the discussion. I felt inadequate, what with Tip's experience and D'Jarl's seven years as a pro. But that was part of what I was supposed to feel. I was learning.

Tip's cell phone rang at the same time as mine. It was Coach Jovanovic connecting a conference call.

"Goot morning," said the coach. "Goot, goot, I catch you both. You have time to see film?"

"Yes," said Tip. "We're here going over our game plan. D'Jarl is with us." Tip put his phone on speaker. I shut mine off.

"I think you want to practice when you get to Spain," said Jovanovic. "I bring the Serbian team over and we scrimmage with you a couple of days. Is right word, ech, scrimmage?"

"It is, and that would be wonderful," said Tip immediately.

Tip gave him the information on the flight we had booked and the hotel we would be staying at. Jovanovic said he would arrange a court to practice on, away from the main venue. Things were not as grim as they had seemed to me just a few hours before.

"Well, that's timely," said Tip.

What Tip didn't mention was that he'd had the foresight to book the flight so the team would arrive three days before our first game. This was to allow our players to get over jet lag. Now our time would be filled with scrimmaging the Serbian team. Damn the jet lag.

The next half hour was spent putting together a practice schedule. D'Jarl would be heavily involved in teaching the international rules. We left Tip's office feeling much better; D'Jarl went to re-tape the different international lane lines on our new practice floor, and I went to check on Norm.

"I have to run home," said D'Jarl. "I'll be back in twenty minutes."

He left me wondering what he was up to, but I didn't have to wait long. He was back, holding a ball, before I could change into my basketball shoes.

"Needs air," he said, bouncing the ball on the floor. It bounced only halfway back to his hand. "International ball," he explained. "It has 12 panels, not eight like ours. A little easier to grip."

"What are the other changes?" I asked.

"Well, the court is three feet shorter and two feet narrower. The 3-point line is closer. Stepping out of bounds for shots from the corner will be our biggest problem. The next difference is going to be on tip-ins and rebounds. Bogdan won't have any problem. Once the ball touches the rim on a shot, international rules allow players to touch it inside the cylinder. We'll have to break Avery, Bingo, and Damari of their instincts, or they will lose a lot of rebounds and give up a lot of points."

Tip came down from his office, walked onto the court, looked at D'Jarl's tape job and the ball that was resting on his hip, and smiled.

We were a lot further along with our team preparations than I was in freeing Stemple.

Norm was reluctant to go to his father's office with the names of the five people we felt were most likely to have committed the murders of Lester Fisher and Madison Francis, Stemple's assistant. Nothing I said would persuade him to come with me. Nate was in court until 4 pm so I knew, what with traffic, I would most likely be later than Michelle in getting home. Nate rolled in at 4:20 and was in a good mood. I suspected he'd left court early and stopped for a couple of snorts.

"These five are the ones who had opportunity and motive, and who are acquainted with the building," I said, handing him

GARY DOC NELSON

the list of George Krusen, John Jensen, Lance LaBarr, Stanford Quoc, and James Tennet.

"What do you mean by motive?" asked Nate.

"All of them were being sued by Fisher and were on Stemple's list of people he's screwed. Norm has talked with all of them except Jensen."

"Alibis?" asked Nate.

"All but Jensen and Quoc, but we haven't firmly confirmed any except LaBarr, who was in the cafeteria with a woman."

"Why's he on the list then?"

"He checks so many of the boxes, Norm thought we should look at him further, despite his alibi."

Nate made a grunting sound that didn't tell me clearly if he approved of Norm's decision or not.

"What do you think?" I asked.

"Any of them might do," said Nate. "Find one who doesn't have an alibi. I can't be blindsided by using someone as an alternate suspect, then have his alibi confirmed. It's impossible to give a jury a second straw man after the first has been discredited."

I knew then that Nate was already in trial mode. He wanted a credible alternate suspect to offer the jury. Norm was sure that Stemple was guilty. I was looking for the real murderer, believing more and more that Stemple had been set up despite all the evidence to the contrary.

"Okay, I'll do a deep look at their alibis."

Nate picked up a file, ending the conversation. I got up and left.

The next day in practice, Tip started by having D'Jarl explain the new court dimensions and the different rules for the European game. When D'Jarl finished, he asked Bogdan, "Have I forgotten anything?"

"When we drive we get extra step," said the Serbian. "Would be called for traveling here."

"Demonstrate," said Tip. "Bingo, you play defense."

I caught Domingo smiling. With his speed and quickness, he was already practicing the move in his mind. It was a good practice. Tip dismissed the team and called a short coaches' meeting, where he gave us our duties for the next four days. I left and went immediately to Norm's office.

Norm wasn't surprised at Nate's reaction the previous afternoon. If anything, he seemed happy that I'd learned the truth about the work we were doing. He'd been busy while I was downtown and at practice and had tracked down John Jensen. Jensen had been in the building the day of the murders, but he'd been in his office with two associates and an assistant. Jensen hadn't been aware of anything until the fire alarm went off. From what he said, the four of them hadn't left each other until they were escorted down in the elevator, kept in the café, then evacuated from the building. Norm had the names of the associates. Of course, there was the possibility that more than one person was involved in the murders, but it seemed like a stretch. Our list of five was now down to three possibles.

Norm was on the phone with one of Jensen's alibis when my cell vibrated. It was Nate.

I quickly told him to cross Jensen off the list, and got a nod from Norm. Evidently the alibi held.

"That's not the worst news," said Nate. I switched my phone to speaker so Norm could hear. "The DA just sent the discovery on the killer's mask over. Hair samples match Stemple's DNA."

"That pretty much seals it," said Norm.

"It's not good," said Nate. "I can argue that it was contaminated when Stemple picked up the mask. I'm having a rush job done on it by our own expert. I should have independent findings tomorrow."

"That's fast," I said. "The DA has had it for what, almost a week?"

"Three days," said Nate. "I pay. I'll get the results faster."

"Do you want us to keep working on the list, or will you ask for a plea?" asked Norm.

"What do you think?" said Nate, his voice showing anger. "Work harder." He hung up.

"So much for presuming Stemple is innocent," said Norm.

I was beginning to think Norm was right. DNA evidence is the hardest to repudiate. It was looking like Stemple had snowed me. How could a man be that manipulative and convincing yet so dumb as to have been caught with fingerprints all over the murder weapon, and to have failed to dispose of his mask? I needed to talk to him more about the mask and his dealings with the suspects still on our list.

CHAPTER 15

When I returned to Norm's small office after practice was over, Norm looked tired. He'd been at the computer for a solid six hours. He might have been trained as an attorney, but it had been a couple of years since he had used those skills. He had never been trained as a PI. I didn't want to verify all his work, but I thought it might be a good idea to double check the alibis.

"Do you have the names of Jensen's alibis?" I asked.

Norm gave me a look–one that said, *I just checked them. He's cleared.*

"I thought I'd check someone you didn't talk to. Just in case there were two people involved in the murders. The likelihood of three is really low."

Norm accepted my explanation and wrote down three names on a scratch pad with a check in front of the one on top. The second on the list was a man named Byron Way. A phone number followed the name.

I phoned Way and made an appointment to see him at his office at 482 Post at 4 pm. I always liked to establish facts in person. A person's body language often says as much as his words. I had an hour to spare. I used it to phone Stanford Quoc, one of those on our list of five likely alternatives. Quoc was free to see me now. His office was at 560 Mission on the fourth floor. The building was beginning to feel like my second home. The streets were relatively clear and I caught every green light. I was parking fifteen minutes after I left the school.

Stanford Quoc was an energetic Asian man of about forty years old. He couldn't be more than five foot six. His office was small, probably one of the smallest in the building. It had a desk facing the entrance and another slightly in back. There was a door that looked like a closet behind the second desk. Each desk had two computer screens set on it and keyboards twice the width of the one I used back at school. Stanford waved me to one of the empty chairs and took the other for himself.

"I've told your associate that I was in my car driving here when the shootings happened," said Quoc in heavily accented English. "I called my office, found out what had happened, turned around, and went home. I don't know much more that I can add."

Quoc's height and heavy accent ruled him out as the gunman, but he did know the building and had had trouble with both Fisher and Stemple.

"I understand you were sued by the man who was killed, and that you had words with Stewart Stemple as well.

"That true," said Quoc. "But that was just business."

"How so?" I asked, noting that Quoc didn't seem upset.

"I set up security for Fisher's office computers. Whole office. He didn't pay me, so I sue him. Him sue me back. Said work was bad, faulty. He crazy. Lose his suit. I win."

"So you got your money?"

"Sure, but spent money fighting his suit. Then he screw me out of getting security contract for entire building. If I had gotten it, security would be better. Police would have murderer by now."

"And why were you mad at Stemple?"

"Fisher hire him to talk with building owners. He do good job for Fisher, bad for building, bad for me."

"Did you know Madison Francis?"

"No. Who she?"

"She was Stewart Stemple's assistant. She was shot and murdered."

"Oh, sorry! No, Fisher and Stemple were just business. It happens all the time in San Francisco, especially when I deal with lawyers. Just business. Nothing to keep mad about."

That might be true, I thought, but having to sue to get money that was owed him and having politics steal a contract seemed like a big deal to me.

Another thought occurred to me, but I wasn't sure how Quoc would react if I asked. "Just between you and me, since you initially installed Fisher's security, did you leave yourself a back door into his database?"

The look I got from Quoc was almost comical. It was flat, the eyes dull, no expression at all. Then he laughed, a high-pitched bark. "Of course. I do in all jobs. Makes it easier to go back and find things for them and correct their mistakes. Don't tell Fisher, though. Customers don't like anyone to have access. Not even person that set up system."

"Fisher's dead. I can promise I won't tell him. So you can look at Fisher's files? Would you be able to do that for me if it would help solve the murder?"

"Maybe. Depends on what you ask," said Quoc, his mouth turning upwards at the corners as if he were considering a final way to get even with Fisher without being sued again.

Even if his height and accent hadn't ruled him out, I would have scratched him off the list just based on his personality and his admission about access to Fisher's files. Now if Franklin Whistel dried up, Nate had another source and another name for his Christmas list.

"One last thing," I said, wanting to know more about the security business. "Your office seems small to handle such big accounts."

Quoc showed that weird corner-of-the-mouth smile again and stood, motioning me to the door behind his desk. He opened it and stepped aside so I could see in. The first thing I noticed was the chill. It had to be ten degrees cooler than the outer office. There were four Asian men sitting behind banks of computers. One entire wall was covered with monitors. "We have two other locations, but this is main one."

"I'm just getting to know about security," I said. "Do you have a locator on your phone?"

"Yes."

"Do you record your phone calls?"

"Yes."

"Could you prove the location of your phone when you made the call to your office?"

Quoc smiled. He knew exactly why I was asking.

"Yes. That no problem. I can give that to you now."

I hoped I hadn't screwed up by asking a security expert and a computer genius to supply his own alibi, instead of asking for his phone and having Nate's crew do it. But I couldn't worry about that now. It was done. Quoc rapidly hit keys on his computer, and almost immediately a printer behind him spat out two sheets. One was a map with a blue dot on a spot about at the intersection of Market and Kearney. It was time stamped. The second sheet was a transcription of his call to the office.

"I transcribe call to office for you," said Quoc. "It was in Tieng Viet. Can give you original if you want."

I thanked Stanford Quoc and told him I wouldn't need the original conversation at this point. I returned to the garage, got into my car, and drove to the 400 block of Polk with at least five minutes to spare for my appointment with Byron Way.

Way's office was as ostentatious as Quoc's was unadorned. An office says a lot about a man. Without even meeting the guy, I pictured him rolling out of the garage downstairs in his Aston Martin. Way was in his late thirties, fit and handsome, dressed in a pair of Levi's and a button-down collared shirt with some logo on the chest that I wasn't familiar with. He might drive an Aston Martin, but at least for this meeting, he seemed like a regular guy.

"What can I do for you?" he asked, his voice as casual as his dress.

I flashed my badge. "I'm working on trying to establish time-lines on the murders that occurred at 560 Mission. I understand you were there."

"I looked you up after you phoned. You're private eye, are you not?"

"Correct. I'm working for an attorney representing one of the individuals who is a suspect."

"I heard the police had already arrested someone."

"That's true. I'm more interested in the timeline of exactly what happened in the building after the shooting. I understand you were there for a meeting with John Jensen?"

"That's correct, two others and me."

"John said that he was with you the entire time, from the first alarm until they let you out of the building. Is that true?"

Way's friendly demeanor changed in a flash. He straightened and pulled back just a fraction. It was exactly why I'd wanted to do the interview in person.

"John's not in any trouble, is he?"

"Not that I'm aware of," I answered. "There's just so much confusion about the time between the first alarm and the second and all the instructions that came over the building's intercom. So John was with you the entire time?"

Way looked conflicted. "Not exactly," he said, finally. "We were working on a project and needed a file that was on the floor below. John left to get it before any commotion happened. If I remember correctly, he returned just after the first fire alarm."

"Do you remember how long that first alarm was on? As I said, I'm working on the timeline before the police arrived."

"It couldn't have been on for much more than a minute. The second one was on for much longer. Then we started to get instructions that there had been a shooting, that when it was safe, everyone in the building would be escorted down to the second floor café–which we were, John included. There was a policeman in the elevator who used a key to operate it. He rode down with us. The cafe was crowded. I shared a table with John and a woman for almost an hour, and then we were allowed to evacuate the building."

"Could you estimate how long John was on the floor below, getting the file?"

Again the show of reluctance. "No more than ten minutes. Maybe less," he added.

I was only five blocks from Nate Hart's office. I called and was in luck. He was still there and would wait for me. After the earthquake in 1906, San Francisco was laid out in a grid with the blocks going east to west, measuring twelve blocks to a mile. I was under half a mile away. I should have been able to get there in six minutes, but the mass of people leaving their buildings at the end of the work day slowed me down. I arrived twelve minutes after I'd called, just before 5 pm.

"What do you have?"

I could tell that Nate was in no mood to extend his work day.

"A couple of things that could be important. I thought you'd want to know immediately. First, put John Jensen back on your suspect list. He lied to Norm about his alibi. He was in the building and unaccounted for at least ten minutes prior to the first alarm."

"He lied to Norm?"

"Yes. He said that he was with a couple of associates the entire time, but one of them admitted Jensen had left to retrieve a file and was not with them until after the first fire alarm. Jensen lied. He might have seen someone while he was getting the file, so there's still work to do. But he did lie."

"Good work," said Nate. "Make sure all the people he was supposed to be with have the same story."

"Also, Stanford Quoc can be dropped from the list. He wouldn't do you any good in court as a straw man. He's only 5'6" and has a heavy accent. No way was he the shooter. His dispute with Fisher came from Fisher not paying him for the security system he set up for the firm. He installed a hidden back way in and can access all the firm's data." I slid the two printouts that I'd gotten from Quoc across Nate's desk.

"This is where Quoc was when he phoned his office during the shutdown of the building, and this is the transcript of the conversation. Both time dated."

"So he gave you this? And told you he has a back door to Fisher's files?"

"I think he sees it as a way of getting back at Fisher for trying to screw him. Oh, and he said that Fisher had used Stemple to botch a deal he had going to supply the security for the entire building. Of course, it concerns me that Quoc is a computer expert and that he provided me with his own alibi."

"I'm going to visit Stemple tomorrow morning," said Nate. "I'll ask him about Quoc. Good work."

He got up and grabbed his coat from the rack behind his desk. I knew when I was dismissed, but then he stopped, turned back to his desk, and took out a thin file.

"This is the DA's analysis report on the ski mask in Stemple's entryway. It's bad." He handed me the file, and this time I was shown out.

I started the five-block walk back to my car. On the way, I decided to start a new, less complicated spreadsheet of our suspects. I would type the five remaining names in green, and I'd list the categories to the right that were causing them to stay on the list. I'd go over my handiwork with Michelle to see if it had any flaws. She often asked questions that made me think of things I'd missed. I was nearing my car when I passed Kalman's flower shop. I stopped and bought a dozen roses for Michelle. With both of us being so busy, it wouldn't hurt to show her how much I loved her.

CHAPTER 16

George Krusen, one of the five men on the list, was a stockbroker. He'd been sued by Fisher for a small amount, but he'd had over five meetings with him over the past month. Whistel told me that a couple of them had involved shouting behind Fisher's closed door. Like most brokers, he started at six and quit at two in the afternoon. I wasn't about to get up at six, so I made an appointment to meet with him at ten-fifteen.

Krusen was a big man, possibly an ex-college football player, with a big smile and a glad-to-meet-you handshake. He was disappointed that I was not there to become a client but to ask questions about the day of the murders.

"I don't know what I can tell you," he said after examining my PI badge and getting the same timeline explanation I had given Byron Way. "I was here, but I didn't learn about the shootings until the alarms and notices started to come through."

"Was anyone with you?"

"No. I manage over five hundred million in accounts. I have an associate who answers the phone and records the transactions, but she was out ill that day."

"I'm trying to nail down the timeline as to what happened that day. The accounts are extremely confused as to alarms and instructions. Could you tell me what you remember?"

"I was on the phone with a client. Saved her over fifty thousand." He had a smug expression that seemed intended to show me how smart he was. "She was going to the south of France for a couple months and wanted to take two hundred thousand out of her account. She wanted me to sell some of her Apple shares. I convinced her to keep those and divest another holding she had in Bosdec. It hadn't done anything since I bought it on her insistence eight months ago. A cousin in Washington had given her a tip that it was about to get a big government contract. It didn't, and had actually lost value. Apple has gained 13 points in the last three days and made her twenty-five percent more than what she took out."

"Wow," I said, unable to disguise my surprise at how casually he threw around numbers that were more than a full year's pay for me. "Do you remember exactly when you started and finished that conversation?"

"Sure. It was before the first alarm. I remember because I was convincing her to divest the Bosdec when the first alarm went off, and it was hard to hear what she was saying. I had to put my end on mute until I wanted to talk."

"This is very helpful," I said. "When did you finish the call?"

"We talked about her trip for a while, then the instructions for evacuating the building came over the speakers and we hung up. I processed the trade before leaving and took the elevator down as instructed. I was held in the café for almost an hour. Did meet a nice lady, though, so it wasn't all time wasted."

"Could you write up what you remember as to the timing of the call?" I asked.

"I can do better than that," he said with that same smug expression. "All trade calls are recorded. I can't divulge the client's name, but you can listen to the entire message, alarms and announcements included in the background. The recording is time logged so you'll know exactly when it happened."

So much for not having a perfect timeline from the sounding of the first alarm. As good as that was, I was almost sorry that it cost us Krusen as a suspect. The guy was so full of himself. Tip had introduced me to a Power 5 basketball coach once who reminded me of Krusen. The coach ran a top-name program that had no problem recruiting. He had a great winning record, but anyone would have with the talent he had. He, like Krusen, had that "I'm me and you're not!" attitude. I would not have invested money with Krusen, even if I'd had it to invest.

"Could I have a copy of that recording?" I asked Krusen. "It would certainly help with the timeline."

"Sure." He took my cell number and transferred the recording with a couple of clicks.

"I'll give you a hundred if you don't tell anyone else you have it or share it with anyone else," I said. For all the guy's big-timing it, he agreed immediately. I copied the recording onto my phone, noting the start time and the finish in my notes, thanked Krusen, gave him a hundred dollar bill, and left. I was wiser but had one fewer suspect.

Norm's notes said that James Tennet, the fourth name on the list, was another attorney. He worked for the firm of Warchec, Bruster, Hannagan, and Dobbs, a personal injury group on the eleventh floor.

It was noted that he'd had a contentious trial against Fisher that had gotten ugly over the jury's award for pain and suffering. He also had a well known dispute with Stemple over an award that was given to the head of a non-profit working with City Hall. It was the easiest of the interviews I'd done so far. If Krusen was a brute, Tennet reminded me of a weasel. He was small with a sliver chin. His front teeth protruded. He wasn't bald, but his hair was so thin that the color of his pale scalp showed through. He was in the building at the time of the murders, but with another dozen lawyers who swore he was at his desk before, during, and after all the alarms and announcements. The group had split into two for the elevator ride to the cafeteria, but other than that, they had been together the whole time.

Nate took personal injury cases but he looked and acted nothing like the group in the Warchec firm. The whole dozen had the same look, as if they would lie when the truth would do just as well. Still, I didn't think they would risk getting caught lying where there were so many others involved. Scratch another name off the list. I had only one more to check, Lance LaBarr. Norm had said that he'd been in the building but had a solid alibi. Our list was shrinking. I needed to go over each of the suspects with Michelle. Maybe she could find another one from our original list of sixteen.

LaBarr also had an office at 560. His was on the 6th floor. There were four people working in what looked like a well set up and efficient space. LaBarr was dressed in a gray suit that looked expensive. He was tall but not as tall as me, and he had brown hair and a well-trimmed mustache. I suspected that the alibi Norm had mentioned was probably like Tennet's, with four other people vouching for him. I was wrong.

"I came in early the day of the shooting," said LaBarr when we sat down in his private office. "Since COVID we usually work from home on Mondays. But I had a handball match at the club at noon, so I had to be downtown anyway."

"Were you in your office when the shooting started?"

"No. I'd finished what I had to do and was in the cafeteria having breakfast when the first alarm sounded. I don't like to eat too much before playing handball."

"Were you there alone?"

"I was when the alarm sounded, but the woman at the next table started to panic, so I joined her. At that point we thought it was a fire."

"So the woman was panicking? Did she calm down?"

"Yep. That is, until the announcement that there had been a shooting."

"I'd be interested in getting her perspective. Did you happen to get her name?"

"Better than that," said LaBarr. He reached into his coat pocket for his wallet. "Got her number. She's cute. I thought of inviting her to dinner, but the way she freaked out made me think twice." He handed me the note with the woman's name and number. I took a picture of it and handed it back.

"Don't say I didn't warn you," said LaBarr. "Skittish women aren't worth the effort."

"I'm set to be married in a month. I'll take your advice, though."

I didn't ask him about his relationship with Fisher or Stemple. If his alibi was soft, there would be plenty of time to go into those.

Julie Wessenberg, the woman whose name was on LaBarr's note, didn't answer her phone, so I left a message. I said that I was an investigator working on the event at 560 Mission and would appreciate a return call.

It was just after noon when my phone rang. She was at her bakery and would be there until two. She asked if I was a reporter.

"No. I'm a private investigator. I'm trying to piece together a timeline, and you could be quite helpful. Could I come and talk to you in half an hour?"

"Yes, but one of my bakers is sick, so I might be helping with a bake, in which case you might have to wait."

"No problem. I'll be there in a few."

It was a strange place to have a bakery, a few blocks away from Union Square, one of the major shopping areas of the city. It had to be convenient, but the rent must surely be high for a commercial bakery.

Julie Wessenberg was behind the counter, which took up a quarter of the store front. The rest was filled with small tables for two, although a couple of them had been pushed together to seat four. She was cute, in a full figured, wholesome kind of way. I introduced myself.

"You're sure you're not a reporter?" she asked, a look of suspicion on her face.

I showed her my PI badge, which seemed to calm her. I could see what LaBarr had meant about her being high-strung. "I understand you were in the cafeteria when the event took place," I said.

"Yes. It was a frightening experience. The paper said that two people were killed."

"When did you arrive at the building?"

"I was in the cafeteria just before the alarm went off. I had an appointment with my accountant and wanted to get there a little early."

"I understand you met a man named Lance LaBarr there."

"Yes. Is that how you got my number? I thought it might be the manager."

"Lance said that you shared a table until the police let people leave."

"That's true. He was eating at a table next to me. I think he could see I was nervous, with all the sirens and alarms and then the announcement that there had been a shooting. Lance was nice enough to sit with me. He was very calm. Said the police were handling it and we were safe."

"And that was just after the first alarm?"

"Yes," said Julie. "I should have known something was up when I heard the police sirens as I entered the building. But they were far away, and you can hear them almost any time in the city."

A voice shouted from the back. Julie turned. "Do you have any other questions? I'm needed in the back."

"This seems like an odd place for a commercial bakery," I said.

"I started it just for the tables here. I've always liked to bake. Then the walk-in trade became busy. A few customers asked if we could supply their lunch rooms, and things just started to expand from that."

Scratch another suspect, along with a five-foot-nothing Vietnamese man, an ex-football lineman, and a lawyer with twelve alibis. It left Jensen, but somehow that didn't seem right either.

I bought half a dozen sweet cakes and croissants to bring to Nate's office. Wessenberg added a thirteenth, to make a baker's dozen. I asked for a second box. A few sweets would go well with yesterday's flowers.

CHAPTER 17

I walked from Wessenberg's bakery to Nate's office. I was getting in my steps. It was not basketball conditioning, but it was better than nothing.

"Be quick," said Nate as I entered his office.

I handed him a copy of the list with the alibis that were confirmed.

"It looks like Jensen is your man. I've checked the alibis of all the others and they look solid. Tennet's were a bunch of lawyers at his firm."

"And you believed them? I wouldn't trust that bunch to tell me if the sun was out."

"I got the same impression, but there were nearly a dozen of them confirming his presence."

"With that much unanimity they must have discussed it before you got there. That lot would argue over the color green."

"Right, but twelve guys lying, it just didn't seem likely. I brought you a box of sweet cakes and croissants," I said, changing the subject and placing the box on his desk, next to the list.

A wave of his hand was my dismissal. I hoped he wouldn't notice that five sweets were missing, safely stored in the spare box I'd gotten from the bakery. I had forty-five minutes before team practice. Already it had been a productive morning.

—

Tip spent an hour practicing jamming rebounds in before they cleared the rim. European rules!

"It's good that we'll have a couple weeks after the trip to break them of this habit," said Tip as we watched.

D'Andre Blaston was fitting in well. He was playing defense on Damari. It was a great matchup. As physically gifted as Damari was, D'Andre's experience from his four years at UConn allowed him to anticipate Damari's moves. The two had bonded, and every score or blocked shot was followed by a hand slap of appreciation for the other's skill. Booker Oowaite was not as advanced as the other bigs. Generally the others were schooling him. D'Jarl was happy to see both the upperclassmen take an interest in showing the incoming freshman what he'd done wrong and how to improve his technique. Booker for his part was a sponge, looking at the two upperclassmen like they were gods.

I worked with Domingo and Jackson Bomar on adding the Euro step in their drives to the basket. I thought it would be easier for them to learn the move than it would be to break them of it later, but it was still not instinctive for them.

Thoughts of the murders kept creeping into my mind as I headed back to my office after practice. I played the recorded conversation that George Krusen had provided again. The murderer, in order to do what he did and get away, had to have not only planned his movements but executed them as precisely as our team was doing Tip's plays. At least now I had an accurate recording and could use it to estimate the time it took to move from floor to floor. Everyone who entered the building had been accounted for by the police in their evacuation. So no one was hiding in the building. We had the name of the killer if it wasn't Stemple. We just didn't know what name.

—

My parents were arriving along with Michelle's for the wedding shower that Janet Dorrinson was holding for Michelle the next day. Lisa Matobi was coming in from Washington, DC as well, but she was staying with Leilah. Everything was set at the house, but there was always something to do, a room to clean or a trip to the store for wine. Both sets of parents had originally planned to rent cars rather than have me pick them up. Once they found that they were arriving within ten minutes of each other, my father quickly suggested that Michelle's dad rent a car that all four of them could use.

Both sets of parents' planes landed on time, Michelle's arriving just before mine. They'd driven through San Francisco and across the Golden Gate Bridge just ahead of me. When I arrived at the house, they had finished unloading the car and were getting set up in the bedrooms. Michelle took them on a short tour, pointing out all the work I'd done since their last visit as well as the jobs she had planned for me in the future. They consisted mostly of landscaping the hill behind the house and, of course, adding a second bathroom. The parents seemed impressed, with my dad asking how much per square foot the bedroom rug had cost. He seemed pleased that we'd bought it as a remnant, avoiding the retail price.

As soon as they were settled and Michelle and the mothers had freshened up, we left in two cars for an early dinner at Marin Joe's. Joe's took no reservations, so it was good that we were eating somewhat early to avoid the wait lines. It was also good because the stomachs of both sets of parents were set to an hour later than ours, standard stomach time.

—

The three men and three women left our house the next morning at 10 am in different cars. The dads went to school to watch morning practice, and the women continued on 101 South toward Woodside. It was a brilliantly sunny day with just a hint of fog visible on the crest of the ridges to the south. The trunk of Michelle's dad's rental was filled with golf clubs. Michelle's Prius was similarly crammed with elaborately wrapped presents.

The Olympic Club was only a twenty-minute drive from the school. It was on a cliff overlooking the Pacific Ocean in the southwest corner of the city. As we drove west from USF, we came to the fog that hugged the coast. I was glad I'd told the dads to bring sweaters.

Our host was waiting for us with an offer of lunch as we pulled into the massive parking lot. We were not about to refuse an Olympic Club lunch and joined our host in the clubroom downstairs overlooking the 8th green. After eating, I still had fifteen minutes to work out any rust that being in basketball preseason had caused my golf game. I excused myself to hit balls on the range.

I ended up shooting a 79. Michelle's dad and our host both shot 78, and Dad survived with a 92 but would have scored much better if he hadn't three putted so many times.

We went in for drinks after the round and were introduced by our host to a number of people. Introductions always started with "I'd like you to meet Rob. He's getting married next month." One drink turned to four, and I was glad that mine were non-alcoholic beers. I'd do the driving home, making sure to use the facilities before we left.

We got to Corte Madera a good half-hour before the women. It was soon apparent that they had topped us in the number of adult beverages consumed. No sooner had they arrived than Michelle asked me to bring the presents in from the car. It was a major task. The trunk and half the back seat were crammed. I piled them all in the front room. While I was unpacking, Leilah and her mom pulled up with another six gifts that wouldn't fit in the Prius. All the seating was taken, so I brought a chair from the kitchen. There were already two bottles of wine open and seven glasses sat filled on the coffee table.

"How many women were there?" I asked, interrupting a giggle from my mom at something Michelle had said.

"Fourteen," answered Michelle. "Mostly Mom's friends, but Janet invited three friends of hers that I hadn't met before."

"They were dear friends by the time we left. I think that was Janet's intention," said Michelle's mom. "They all seemed interested in Michelle's role as head of the Dorrinson Foundation. Janet made it sound like Rob had saved the foundation's $28 million and caught the murderer all by himself."

"He almost did," said Michelle. "The policemen in charge kept insisting that it was another man even after the real murderer confessed."

"Did I get my saber saw?" I asked in jest, looking at the pile in the center of the room and trying to change the subject. This elicited a peel of laughter from the ladies and smiles from both the dads.

The women sipped their wine and Mrs. DelCarlo started reading from a notebook. Leilah had recorded what Michelle said when each present was opened. For some reason all three ladies thought the remarks were hilarious. I just wondered what we would ever use some of the stuff for, and more importantly, where we would store it.

"We arrived perfectly, fifteen minutes late," said Michelle's mom. "Everyone was already there and on their first drink."

Something in the way she said it triggered a shadow thought that had been sitting in the back of my brain. I came close to pulling it to light but wasn't successful. It kept hovering like the sun behind a cloud.

"Do you like the color of the towels?" asked Michelle.

I knew it was useless to try to remember what it was now, and sat back and enjoyed the women as they relived every gift. At last there was only one gift left, one to Michelle from Leilah. Michelle opened it slowly. Wrapped in light blue tissue paper was a Skil saber saw. Everyone laughed, including me. My ignorant comment had turned into a joke on me, but it had gained me a saw.

Both sets of parents left the next day. I cooked breakfast for them and helped pack their rental car. Michelle and I were finally alone at eleven-thirty. The house almost echoed with the silence, a testament to how much activity there had been over the previous day and a half. I realized that Michelle was due to have two more showers, one for her friends and another in Texas with my mom's friends. I thought I'd better build a storage room along with the second bathroom. At least I would be in Europe with the team when those showers were held. I hoped I'd be able to move through our living room when I got back.

As important as the shower was to Michelle, my own thoughts kept returning to the Stemple case. Nate was due for a preliminary hearing soon. He wouldn't offer up Jensen at that point, but he'd find out what the DA had as evidence beyond what we already knew. I remembered that I still hadn't read the file on the findings about the mask. I left Michelle, still touching each gift with wonder, and went to my den. It was still set up as the bedroom my parents had used, so I took some time stripping the bed and returning it to its usual function. I figured I could score a few points by doing the same with Michelle's parents' room, so I did that one as well and started the washing machine.

"I was going to do that," said Michelle, coming up behind me and giving me a hug. "I never asked how you played yesterday."

"We had fun," I said, side-stepping the question. "The Olympic Club is a special place. But it's not nearly as nice for a wedding as the Meadow Club. I'm glad we're getting married there."

"Several of the ladies asked if we were members," said Michelle.

"Don't get any ideas," I replied. "Both clubs have hefty entry fees, and besides, our host at the Meadow Club said there was a seven-year waiting list. Would you do the second load? I have something I have to read on my desk."

She gave me a long kiss. "My dad said you should apply to the club and get on the waiting list. He has the sponsors lined up."

My mind didn't work seven years ahead, let alone my pocket-book. I let the suggestion go and went back to my den.

CHAPTER 18

The DA's discovery report on the mask found just outside Stemple's office looked both thorough and official. Looking at it, I wished Mike Ronning was back from his vacation. Mike had much more experience looking over court documents than I did. The report consisted of a summary and photos, followed by a detailed scientific explanation of the tests that had been performed. As I read the summary, the evidence seemed conclusive. They had recovered hair from the inside of the mask. It had been tested and was a confirmed DNA match to Stemple at 99.996%. There were a number of pictures–of the cap, a close-up of the fibers showing a hair, and a few of the recovered hairs on a white paper background. I wanted to be in court when Nate the Great explained this.

Following the summary and pictures was a detailed report on the items, the tests performed, and the findings. Much of it was in scientific jargon and expensive words that I knew were used to underline the qualifications of the state's expert witness and impress a jury. I felt I was wasting my time until I came to the description of the hair. There were sixty-three individual strands. This struck me as a lot of hair. I went back to the pictures.

I got up and went to the front room, where Michelle was watching TV after starting the second load of sheets.

"Honey, would you please read this report from the DA and tell me if you see anything strange?"

Michelle took her time. When she got to the end, where the description of the hairs was given, she stopped, looking up wide-eyed. "That's an awful lot of hair for trace evidence. The photo of the hair on the paper shows only two strands, and it isn't a close-up. Then later it says that there are sixty-three strands."

"I took a photograph of the picture on my phone and magnified it," I said. "Nate might do something with this after all. I need to talk to Stemple in the morning. We might just have earned my salary."

The next morning I painted the shelves in my closet, then left for the San Francisco jail for a ten o'clock meeting with Stemple. On the way I phoned Nate's office and left a message with Linda concerning the recording I'd bought from Krusen.

Maybe they were getting tired of me pulling Stemple out of his cell. Maybe it was just that today's crew was slower. This time I had to wait for over half an hour to be led to the interview room.

"I need the name of your barber and any other place where you cut your hair," I said, before Stemple could start complaining about still being in jail.

"What's Hart doing? I haven't seen him in almost a week."

"He's working to get you out. He has some good things to tell you when he's able. Stay calm and be patient. The information you've been giving me has been very helpful. What's your barber's name?"

"Randolph Forsythe."

"You've got to be kidding. That's a name? Is he a movie star?" I asked.

"I think he was in the movies once." Stemple wrote the name and address down. Having gotten what I needed, I got up to leave.

—

I wanted to see Nate as soon as possible. Soon wasn't possible. When I arrived at his office, he was occupied with a client. I waited and spent the time talking with Linda, his legal secretary. She was a nice-looking girl. She was the type of woman I might have dated, but Michelle and I had met and all such thoughts had gone out the window. I always got the impression when in Nate's office that she liked me as well. Too bad. I was fully in love with Michelle before I'd met Linda.

It was just short of an hour before Nate's door opened and his client emerged. I couldn't tell if he was happy with the meeting or mad. His face was as stoical as an Easter Island statue.

Nate was surprised to see me and looked inclined to go straight back to his office.

"I think the DA is trying to pull a fast one on you," I said quickly.

Nate stopped and turned back. "How long?"

"For what I found, ten minutes. But you might have some questions."

"In!"

"The report on the mask," I said, putting the document on his desk. "Deliberately or not, the DA's hiding something. First, the photos of the hair samples have no close-ups. And the shot shows only two strands. When you get to the fine print, it says that there were a total of sixty-three. It seems like an awful lot of hair to come from the inside the mask. I magnified the shot of the three hairs and could find no follicles, just hair. I checked. Most hair that is lost naturally has part of the follicle attached. I suspect that these were cut. There is no mention in the report of the missing follicles or the oddity of the large number of hairs."

"Not only is this interesting, but I can nail her in trial for withholding evidence. It would depend on the judge, but a jury would eat it up."

"This morning I visited Stemple. I figured the only way he would lose that much hair is if he just had a haircut. He hasn't had one in over two weeks. And he showers and shampoos every day. I suspect that if you ask your own testing experts, they'll find that the ends of the hairs were cut, therefore likely planted. I've got the name of Stemple's barber but haven't contacted him for a statement yet. I thought you'd like to know before your experts finish their examination of the mask."

"You did right," said Nate, slamming his fist on the file.

"I was thinking that they have the clothes Stemple was wearing the day of the murder. We could test the shirt for loose hairs. If there are none, it would make it even more likely that the samples in the mask were planted."

"I'll get it done," said Nate, smiling. "If there's no hair on the clothes, it's another rip in the DA's case."

"I just thought of it, but we have only Stemple's word that the murderer was wearing that particular mask, not him. If Stemple is telling the truth, why is there no evidence of the real murderer's DNA on it?"

Nate's smile disappeared. "Keep it up." He turned back to his desk, where there was another file opened, probably from the man who had just left.

I'd thought of a number of things during my talk with Nate. Most importantly, I had to talk with Stemple's barber and find out who would have the opportunity to collect his cut hair. Hurry up and come back, Mike Ronning! For the first time since I'd been given the job, I really thought Stemple might be innocent. I was pretty sure that it would take more to convince Norm, but it was enough to give him some doubt.

—

Norm wasn't at his desk when I got to school just after eleven. I left a Post-it asking him to phone me when he arrived and went to my own office. I'd barely opened my email file of recruits for the following year when my phone rang. It was Norm. He was in his office.

Norm and I had made the rounds after he'd passed the Bar. He was always a little more into the nightlife than I was. Now, looking at him, I suspected that he hadn't changed. I didn't think it was possible to lose a tan over a weekend, but that's what it looked like Norm had done. His eyes were rimmed with red and if a 30-year-old could have bags, he had them.

"Looks like you could use some lunch," I said.

"You mean breakfast."

"You can tell me about it over food. I'll drive."

I took Norm to Mel's on Geary Street. It's only six blocks away from school. Straight streets and only two turns, which I took slow. I didn't want any mishaps for the otherwise clean interior of my old Camry. I was glad I'd left the Viper at home.

I had a Mel's burger. Norm had a stack of pancakes, sausages, and two tall glasses of orange juice. Halfway through the meal, some of his color returned.

"Do you remember Eve Hoversal?" he asked, sopping up syrup on a large wedge of pancake.

"Sure, who wouldn't?"

"We spent the weekend together. I didn't realize she was as wild as she is."

"Didn't she get married?" Eve had been every boy's dream in high school: blond, beautiful, with a rich father who gave her a new Mercedes the day she got her license. I always thought that she kind of looked down her nose at boys our age.

"She did. Lasted two years. Now she's single again. Says she's an independently wealthy ex-married woman."

"Good to hear, at least for you. I've got work for you when you feel up to it."

"The Stemple case?" asked Norm, stuffing the last of the tall stack of pancakes into his mouth.

"Yup."

I was worried what Norm would think when I told him that Jensen's alibi wasn't solid, like he'd told me. I'd thought hard on how to break it to him that he'd been misled. I'd decided that the best way to handle it was to be straightforward.

"Don't tell me he was lying about being with two associates and an assistant?" asked Norm.

"Partly. He was with them, but he left to get a file. He was out of their sight from before the first alarm until the second, ten minutes and nineteen seconds in total."

"Shit. I'm sorry. I thought he wouldn't lie when three people could back him. It was why I only interviewed one of them. Did I screw up any of the others?"

"No. Tennet is like Jensen. He was with a dozen lawyers in his firm. Nate doesn't trust them, but they all give the same story. Quoc has a solid alibi, plus he's short and has a thick accent. I talked with the woman LaBarr was with in the cafeteria. His alibi is solid, just like you said. Get this, though–George Krusen was on the phone making a trade the entire time, from before the first alarm until the announcement to evacuate to the lower floors. He has it all on a recording. That's how I know exactly how long Jensen was gone. I bought the recording for Nate. I hope I didn't pay too much."

"Don't worry about that. It will just go on Stemple's bill," said Norm, looking a lot better after the food and the news that he'd only dropped the ball on one of the five. "Where do we go from here?"

I told him about the DA's report on the hair from the mask and the inconsistencies.

"You have been busy," said Norm.

"So have you if what you say about Eve Hoversal is true."

"Yeah, but I won't be able to charge it to Stemple's account."

"I recorded all the interviews. I'll send them to you," I said. "See if there's anything I missed. I'll take the barber."

"Done. Thanks for the breakfast."

CHAPTER 19

Randolph Forsythe's shop was on the seven hundred block of Geary. It had a pink and yellow awning. The color scheme inside matched. There were four chairs. Three of them were occupied by three hairdressers, a better term than barber. All of them were looking at me, their work momentarily suspended.

"Randolph?"

"Yes. Do you have an appointment?" asked the man in the farthest chair.

"No, I don't. I'm a private investigator working on a case that involves one of your clients. It would help if you could answer some questions. It will only take a minute and it's very important."

The sound of scissors snipping stopped. From the looks on the faces of all three behind the chairs, I could tell they thought I was there to count towels to tell how many cash customers were being left off the books to avoid taxes.

"Can you wait? I'm almost finished here."

I nodded and took a seat in front. Minutes later, the customer Forsythe was working on came to the front desk, followed by Forsythe. Cash was exchanged. Forsythe made a point of giving the man a receipt. The guy looked at it, clearly not expecting it, and left.

"You say you're a PI. What has this got to do with me?"

"You have a client, Stewart Stemple. I was wondering if you could tell me when you last cut his hair."

If the scissor clipping had paused before, now it came to a dead stop.

"Oh God! Stewart!" said Forsythe. "July 2nd. How could I forget?"

"Is there somewhere private you could tell me about it?" I asked. Obviously there was more to the story than just the date.

"Everyone here knows about it already," said Forsythe. "Stewart is somewhat demanding. He always wants the last appointment or asks me to stay late. He had the last appointment on July 2nd but showed up almost half an hour late. I waited. I shouldn't have."

"What happened?"

"You don't know? You're not here because of it?"

"I don't know what 'it' is."

"Well." He drew out the word like it was a sentence. "I had just finished Stewart. He's quite picky. He wants to look like he hasn't had a haircut. At least he schedules after his workouts, so his hair is always freshly washed."

"What happened?" I interrupted, thinking that Forsythe might take forever to get to the point.

"I was almost murdered. That's what happened. I was alone working on Stewart. Everyone else had cleaned up and left. Stewart gave me a nice tip and just as he left, another man came in. His hair looked like it had been cut with a hedge clipper. I was immediately afraid. He pulled out a knife and pushed me to the back of the shop. He had me lie face down on the floor. It was filthy. I hadn't swept up after Stewart yet. He cut me with his knife. Made me bleed." He pointed to a red mark on his neck about a quarter-inch long. "He went through my pockets and took my entire day's cash, just over eight hundred dollars. He told me to stay on the floor for five minutes. That he would be watching from his car and would come back if I moved."

"Did you see whether he took some hair from the floor?"

"No. I told you I was face down. Why would he do that?"

"Did he have time to do it?"

"I guess. I couldn't see what he was doing before he searched me."

"Can you describe him?"

"I gave all this to the police on the night it happened. Even looked at a bunch of photos."

"Yes, but I'd like to hear it from you." Nate's Christmas list was about to get bumped up again, but I knew he could get a copy of the police report.

"He looked like a street tough. I told you his hair was terrible. It was black. He had black eyebrows and a scar on the bridge of his nose like he'd been in a fight. Had a chipped front tooth. He was about my height, strong, five-ten, and had a tattoo on his left arm, but I didn't have time to see anything about it, other than it was blue."

"Eye color?"

"I think they were brown, but it was his eyebrows that caught my eye. They really needed to be plucked."

"Anything else you can tell me about him? Maybe something that you forgot to tell the police?"

"Well. . ." There it was again, a full sentence. "From the way he searched me, he wasn't gay."

It was as much as I was going to get. Both the other cutters and their clients were laughing behind Forsythe. I gave him my card, thanked him, and started to leave.

"Eight hundred dollars," I said out of curiosity. "Quite a good day's work. How much do you charge for a haircut?"

"Ninety dollars plus tip. You find that thief and I'll do you for free."

I left, knowing that I probably wouldn't take him up on his offer.

—

I phoned Norm. He was still at his desk at school. I asked him to stay put and told him I'd be there in ten minutes. I wasn't Tip Pennington early, but I still entered Norm's small room eight minutes after I'd called. Norm looked considerably better. There were two cartons of orange juice open on his desk and three cans of Diet Coke. I guess he was still rehydrating from his weekend with Eve Hoversal.

"You look like somebody goosed you with a feather," said Norm. "What's up?"

"And you don't look like you spent the evening with Dracula anymore. Nice to see some color in your face. Good news, I think. I followed up with Stemple's barber, guy named Randolph Forsythe."

"For real?"

"For real. Turns out Stemple had his hair cut almost two weeks before the murders." I told Norm about the circumstances of the robbery and that there had been an opportunity to collect Stemple's hair.

"Will this guy be a credible witness for Nate if it goes to trial?"

"I think so. At the very least he'll be entertaining. We find the guy who robbed him and you get a free haircut."

"Was he able to give you a description?"

"A good one. Five-ten, dark unkempt hair, black eyebrows in need of a plucking," I chuckled. "Has a chipped front tooth, scar on his nose, possible tattoo on his left arm in blue ink. Took eight hundred off him using a knife. Forsythe said the guy was probably in his thirties and looked like a street person."

"Nate can get the police report," said Norm, with conviction. "Had the police been to see Forsythe since the robbery?"

"Sounded like they saw him at the time of the robbery, but it didn't seem like they've followed up. I could check."

"Don't," said Norm. "Nate can find out. If they haven't, then they haven't connected the dots. The haircut to the hair found in the mask. Either they've missed it or the DA is holding back because of the snag it puts in her case against Stemple. My guess is that the police haven't been told that it was Stemple whose hair was cut, since he'd left before the robbery."

"It's still pretty tenuous that the robbery of a beauty parlor and the murder at 560 Mission are connected." Nate could make it look like there was a direct connection, but it could be taken as a mere coincidence. I told Norm so.

"You just gave me an idea," said Norm. "And I have some time."

"Time for what?"

"Time for the other thing the police haven't connected to the murders–my car break-in."

"How does that help?"

"The day after it happened I checked for any surveillance cameras."

"Yes, you said there were none."

"There were none on my car, but there were some on the corners. I looked at them, but I didn't know the exact time my car was busted into, and I didn't know who I was looking for. I'm going back to look at the cameras again now that I have a description."

"If you can connect the robbery to your car break-in, Nate really has a chance of convincing the court that somebody other than Stemple is behind the murders."

"You know, the reason I don't like criminal law is that more often than not, Nate is trying to get a guilty person off or at least get him a reduced sentence. Don't feed me the 'Every person is entitled to representation' bullshit. I'm even beginning to think that Stemple might be innocent. I would even watch this one if it came to trial, just to see Nate take the DA apart."

"You might want to check for cameras on the seven hundred block of Geary as well. South side of the street. I don't know if they would keep the footage for two weeks, but if they did, they might give you a picture of the thief. I'll ask Nate about sending a sketch artist to Forsythe, but he might not want to alert the police as to what we know about the hair."

The day ended better, much better for both of us. I decided to celebrate by taking Michelle out to dinner. Before I left school, I stopped by my own office. I was surprised to see Tip's office door open. Not a good sign. Tip was sitting at his desk, looking at his computer.

"I guess you didn't check your email today," said Tip as I entered.

"I did this morning, but I've been busy," I said, wondering what I'd missed.

"Simu Vuksan has broken his wrist."

"How?" I immediately knew that wasn't the right question. I should have asked how badly.

"He fell during a league game. Fractured his ulna, near the wrist, and chipped the lunate carpal bone."

"Which hand?" Broken hands were common in basketball and always a concern.

"The left. His shooting hand," said Tip.

I quickly went through the months until pre-conference started. "That gives us three and a half months for him to heal before the games start."

"I'm not worried about that. I'm worried about who will set it and what kind of job they'll do. I wouldn't be concerned if we had our doctor doing it."

"Could we have him come over and have the procedure done here?" I asked.

"Already asked," said Tip. "His father is friends with a surgeon over there and wants him to set it."

"I can see why you're concerned. You want me to check the doctor out?"

"That's what the email I sent you is about. I'm trying to get a line on him from our orthopedic guys."

"I can do that." I could. I felt the stress building. The Stemple case, the wedding, now this.

In my office, I looked up the number of Dr. Shimizu, our orthopod. He and his partner Dr. Buxton were on contract with our school. One had to attend every home basketball game and was on call for all the other sports. He answered on the third ring.

"Yes, Coach."

"We have a problem that we don't know how to handle and hoped you could give us some guidance."

"What's the problem?"

"A five-star recruit that we signed for next year fell and broke his wrist. Broke the ulna and chipped his lunate bone. Our problem is that he's Serbian and his father, who's a lawyer, has a doctor friend that he wants to set it. It might need a screw," I said, reading the email that Tip had forwarded to me. "We were wondering if you could look at the X-rays. Tip would hate to see this kid's future ruined if the procedure was done poorly."

"Sure. I can look at it, see the X-rays, and talk to the physician."

"I don't even know if he speaks English," I said. "We just found out about this a couple hours ago."

I forwarded the email, which was now compiling a pretty good string, and thanked Dr. Shimizu. As I was shutting down my computer, I heard Tip's door close.

"Dr. Shimizu is checking on things," I said. Tip and I walked to our cars together.

I phoned Michelle once I left the garage. I needed a night out as much as Michelle.

CHAPTER 20

I decided to get to school early, and I called Nate on the way in. It was one of the few times of the day when I was sure of getting through to him, as he was driving into his office as well.

"Speak." Nate was Nate.

"Things are beginning to break," I said. I quickly told him about Stemple's barber and the robbery.

"So the robber had the opportunity to grab some hair?"

"Yes. Cut hair. He also threatened the hairdresser with a knife. We have a good description of the guy. Norm's going back to look at the security film around the area where his car was broken into now that we know what the guy looks like."

"Good idea. It would tie the guy to the case. Norm thought of that?"

"Yes."

"Tell Norm good work." Nate hung up.

I'd no sooner sat down at my desk than my phone rang. I was so used to my cell that I automatically looked at it before realizing that the one on my desk was the one ringing. It was Dr. Shimizu.

"Rob?"

"Yes. Good morning, Doc."

"I've looked at the X-rays of Simu Vuksan. It's a typical break when someone lands on his palm. You should tell him not to try to break his falls with his hand. Use his butt, his arm, anything but his hand."

"How does it look? Is it serious?"

"The ulna sheared up from the wrist joint. That's actually better than if it had broken at right angles to the length of the bone. It gives more surface to join. Easier to put two pins in for stabilization as well. The doctor in Serbia has already done the surgery. I've seen the post op X-rays. Looks excellent. I'd say he's in good hands."

"Will he have to have the pins removed?"

"Typically no. Two months in a cast, then another month in a soft cast, and he should be good to go. You say he's a five-star recruit?"

"Yes. Tip will be happy with this news."

"I'll look forward to watching him play."

I went online and looked up the wrist and forearm on Wikipedia. The ulna was really small compared to the radius. The metacarpals looked like a bag of marbles.

It wasn't even 9:45 and it was already a good day. I hung up and immediately there was a knock on the door. It was Norm.

"I heard you talking. It sounded official," said Norm as I waved him inside.

Norm sat and tossed two pictures across my desk. "I checked out the security cameras last night. The one on the west corner hadn't kept the film. They recycle every three days, but the east corner caught this."

The first shot was of a man wearing a hoodie, his face partially hidden. The second was of the same guy looking up, his face clear if somewhat fuzzy. "It was taken fifteen minutes after I left my car to go back to 560."

"Nate has a guy who can sharpen that up," I said.

"Might not need to," said Norm. "Have you read the paper this morning?" He handed me his phone. It had the Chronicle website pulled up and an article centered. A man had been shot in a robbery of a mom-and-pop grocery store in the outer Richmond district last night. It had a description of the robber: black hair, bushy eyebrows, scar on his nose, and a chipped front tooth. The police were asking people with information about the robbery to please contact them.

"Sounds like our guy. I thought you might like to take a ride to the Richmond district this morning."

"Says that the proprietor was shot."

"Wana bet that a .380 caliber bullet was used?"

"No bet," I said. "Let's take a ride."

The Outer Richmond, 40th Avenue and Geary to be exact, was a straight drive down Fulton, then a right on 40th. Norm drove. It took less than ten minutes. The store was on the corner. It was easier to find than a parking place. Inside there was a young Asian man behind the counter. He was wearing a blue suit and looked like he didn't belong.

"I'm Rob MacKay, I'm an investigator." I flashed my badge. "I'd like to ask a few follow-up questions about the robbery and shooting last night."

"I wasn't here. It was my grandfather, Simon Wong, who was shot."

"Is he going to be all right?" asked Norm, taking the lead.

"He's out of critical care, if you call getting shot in the chest all right."

"I need to view the security tape," I said, trying to sound official.

"We have two of them, one at the front door and one at the counter. The police took copies yesterday."

"I need to see the original footage."

"But you already have it." The guy was getting nervous.

"Show him the street shot," I said to Norm.

"We think we know the shooter. We just want to compare what you have on the original," said Norm, showing the man the picture on his phone of the suspect in the hoodie on the street near his car.

"That's him," said Simon Wong's grandson. He had obviously seen the tape.

"Fantastic. Now could we look at your security footage?"

"I have to be at the counter. Can you wait for someone to relieve me?"

"How long will it take?"

"Not long. Maybe ten minutes."

"Fine," said Norm. "We don't need the whole film copied. Just a minute or so."

A few minutes after the call was made, the entrance door chimed and a middle-aged man, also in a blue suit, came in, went directly to the counter, and spoke in Chinese to Wong's grandson.

"My son tells me you found the shooter."

"We don't know his name yet. We do know that he's connected with another crime. Your security tape will help us identify him," I said.

He nodded, led us to a small crowded room at the back of the store, and showed us how to access the surveillance tape.

There were several places in both films that had clear images of the robber. We both took photos on our cell phones. It took less than five minutes. We heard the door chime three times while we worked. When we came out, there was a customer just picking up her bag.

"I don't see why you police officers can't work together," said the grandson from behind the counter. "You already have the entire film."

"I'm not with the police," I said quickly. "I'm a private investigator." I pulled out my wallet and gave a business card to each of them. "Both the police and I are working to find the guy who shot Mr. Wong. The more people looking, the better the chance of getting him. Thank you for your cooperation." I could see he had more questions. I nudged Norm toward the door and we left.

"What now?" asked Norm as we climbed into his car.

"We get to school and wait for the shit to hit the fan."

It didn't take that long. We were just passing through Park Presidio Drive on Fulton when my phone chimed. It was Inspector Philip Farley. I was pleased that he was the one to call. I was surprised that he'd done it so quickly.

"Inspector, good to hear from you. I'm driving. Could you call me in ten minutes? I'll be at school then."

"I'll do better than that. I'll meet you there in half an hour."

"We have new offices. They're upstairs over the new Malloy practice court."

"Fine." He hung up. He was mad. I didn't care.

I heard the knock on the office's outside door. I'd left my door open so I wouldn't miss it. Farley was true to his word. It was less than half an hour after he'd called.

We'd worked together on two murders in the two and a half years that I'd been working for Nate. Both had been solved with Farley getting much of the credit, along with a promotion to inspector. I figured I had a little goodwill banked from the help I'd given the police in those cases. The way Farley was acting, it didn't look like it.

"Interfering with an ongoing investigation is a serious crime," said Farley.

"Are you referring to the shooting of Simon Wong?"

"You know I am. What were you doing there looking at the security footage?"

"I was doing exactly what the police asked for in this morning's paper."

"Providing information is not the same as looking at classified evidence."

"First of all, no one said it was classified. Not the shop owners, no tape or notice on the film. The grandson had even seen the tape, for Christ's sake. I identified myself as an investigator and showed my badge. I even gave my card to both of them. Secondly, I didn't know for sure that I had any useful information about the robber until I saw the film."

"They said you had a picture of the perp," said Farley, calming down a little.

"Yes, that's what made us want to see if it was the same guy. That, and the fact that he used a gun."

"If you had your suspicions, why didn't you bring us the picture?"

"I thought you might already have it. You would if your department did its job."

"Don't be a wise ass. Where did you get the picture?"

"A week ago, my friend's car was broken into. His Colt Mustang six shot was stolen out of a locked trunk. It was registered and legal. Not a word from the police since, except for the DA trying to charge my friend for not securing his weapon."

"It was the story in the paper, that someone had been shot. I wondered if it could have been the same guy using my friend's gun. Our picture came from a corner security camera where his car was parked." I opened my desk and took out the picture I'd shown Wong's grandson. "It's the same guy, and I bet the slug that got Mr. Wong is a .380."

"All right," said Farley, a lot friendlier than he'd been when he entered. "Who is your friend?"

"Norm Hart."

"Hart, the attorney's son?"

"Yes, we've been friends since high school."

"Was he the one with you this morning?"

"Yes. I suppose you'll want his number?" A nod from Farley and I wrote Norm's number on a scratch pad.

"MacKay, I have a lot of respect for your ability as a PI. Let's keep it that way. Do you know who this guy is?" Farley waved the picture at me.

"In both pictures, the guy's wearing gloves. I suspect that means that his prints are on file somewhere. Someone knows who he is. I hope that this cooperation you talked about means you'd give me access, should you find him before we do?"

"This is different. Before, you were working for a private party and the Warriors. Now you're working for Nate Hart, a defense attorney. That puts you and me on different teams. Again, leave this to the police."

"I'd like to be kept in the loop so I don't have to bring the Feds into it." The FBI had taken part in both cases the previous two years. Farley had played nice, as did the federal agents, but nothing bothers a local cop more than the FBI coming in and big footing a case. Farley grunted.

"Not going to happen." He got up and left. I was more than happy that Farley was assigned to the case. He was smart and a square shooter. Knowing each other would make it a whole lot easier dealing with him, even with his attitude about defense attorneys. We needed to make a stronger connection between the guy in the picture and the 560 murders. The theft of the file was not enough. It was a thin thread that any prosecutor could snap in a second.

I phoned Nate for the second time in four hours. I would probably catch him at lunch, which wouldn't bother Nate, as he would be able to charge it to Stemple in billable hours.

I told him about the article in the Chronicle and what Norm and I had done. The best part was how we'd matched the description of the hairdresser's robber to that of the grocery store shooter and Norm's car break-in.

"When we got back to school Inspector Farley came to see me. He's not thrilled with what we did. Cited obstructing a police investigation. He's also not real happy that you're involved."

"Fuck him," said Nate. "Text me the photos."

I did what he asked.

"Hold on." No explanation, just the order. I sat in silence for over a minute.

"Call this guy," said Nate, giving me a name and a number. "Take Norm with you when you meet him. He might be able to put a name to the pictures. The guy only had one name, Carlos."

I went down the stairs to Norm's office, told him about Farley and what his father had said, and made the call. It was short and sweet. I mentioned Nate, and we arranged to meet at a restaurant at 2034 Mission in an hour.

"Feel like lunch?" I asked Norm. He shrugged his assent.

The restaurant was the only one of the four on the street that didn't serve Mexican food. We arrived fifteen minutes early and ordered food; Norm, a Cobb salad with chicken, and a hamburger for me.

At exactly the arranged time, a man came in and took a seat at the counter. He had dark hair worn long and a dusky complexion. He was wearing jeans and a black tee shirt. His back was to us but I saw heavy tattoos extending from the edge of his shirt up to behind his ears. I could see he was looking at us in the mirror behind the counter. When our food arrived, he got up and sat at our table.

"Nate send you?"

"Yes. Carlos?" A nod of the head was his answer.

"Nate thought you might know this person or could find out what his name is." I slid two photos from the Richmond shooting across the table.

Carlos pulled them close to his chest so that no one could see what he was looking at from behind him. "It's important to Nate?"

"Very," I said.

"The phone you called me on still good?"

"Yes, or you could tell Nate directly."

"Give me twenty dollars," said Carlos.

I got out my wallet and gave him twenty. Carlos looked at the counter, then slipped me two packs of sugar, closing my fingers around them.

Carlos folded the pictures to a size that fit in his pocket, got up, and left without a word, leaving the Coca-Cola he had brought from the counter untouched.

"That was weird," I said as I picked up my hamburger, wondering how I was going to fit it in my mouth.

Norm looked at me, confused.

"The sugar?"

"He wanted it to look like you were scoring. That wouldn't raise an eyebrow around here. Carlos helping us find our guy would."

I put the sugar packets in my jacket pocket and attacked my hamburger.

We'd just arrived back at school and were sitting in Norm's office when my phone rang.

"Guy's name is Buddy Doyle. No address. He moves around Castro and Ingleside districts. Small time. Deals some meth. Does some strong arm stuff. You never met me." Carlos hung up.

Norm looked at me. I was hurriedly writing down what had been said. "Better tell Nate."

CHAPTER 21

Nate might be getting tired of taking my calls, but it was still early in the afternoon. I didn't think he'd be upset at the information I had for him. I left the speaker on so Norm could hear.

"Carlos came through," I said quickly, before Nate could give his usual cheery greeting. "Guy's name is Buddy Doyle. He runs in the Castro and Ingleside districts. No address."

"Call Inspector Farley right now and give him the name."

"Farley made it real clear that I couldn't have access to the guy. I don't think giving him his name will change his mind."

"Let me worry about that," said Nate.

"What do you think Nate has up his sleeve?" I asked Norm when Nate hung up.

"Smoke and mirrors. Smoke and mirrors," said Norm with a wide grin.

Norm watched as I phoned Farley and gave him Buddy Doyle's name. I left the speaker on but there wasn't much to hear. Farley asked me to repeat the name and hung up. No thank you. No "Where did you get the information?" I wondered if he took lessons from Nate.

I'd almost forgotten to tell Tip about Simu's surgery. I left Norm, went upstairs to Tip's office above the practice court, and knocked.

"Good news," I said as I walked in. "Dr. Shimizu checked out the Serbian doctor and said he's top notch. Trained in the United States. Not only that but the surgery is already done. Two pins. Doc says he's seen all the X-rays and it looks great. Three months. Two months in a hard cast and another in a soft one."

"I got a call from Coach Jovanovic an hour ago," said Tip. "He said the same thing."

"Dr. Shimizu gave me the information a couple of hours ago," I said, hoping to explain the time it had taken me to report it to Tip. "I wanted to look up the medical terms so I seemed more knowledgeable about what he'd told me." I had, but it had been the day before.

Norm pushed away from his desk as I walked into his office.

Norm smiled and leaned back in his chair. "What now, boss?"

"We wait until Farley picks up Buddy Doyle. I don't know how we'll get access to him. I'm sure the police will focus on the shooting and not the car break-in. It's just the opposite for us."

"Nate said not to worry about it, so don't worry about it," said Norm.

"I think we've gone as far as we can go on the information we have," I said. "Would you like to join Michelle and me for dinner?"

"Sure. Can I bring a date?"

"Eve Hoversal?" I asked, already knowing the answer.

"Yeah. We were going out this evening already."

"Sure. How about Antonio's at 2nd and Clement?"

"Time?" asked Norm.

"5:30. It's early, but Michelle works in the city now and leaves at five."

"Done."

I remembered what Norm had said about Eve being wild. It was sure to be an interesting evening.

Michelle was happy to eat out. We'd been to Antonio's two years ago, when we had met Nate Hart for dinner. Great Italian food, and a staff that treated Nate like royalty.

Michelle met me at school and we drove in one car to the restaurant, where parking was difficult. I told the woman at the front desk that we were meeting Norm Hart, and she showed us to the same table in the back that we'd had when we ate with Nate. Evidently the name Hart carried weight through the generations. While we were waiting, I told Michelle that Eve had been a classmate of Norm's and mine in high school. Seeing Michelle's raised eyebrow, I quickly added that we had never dated, and the eyebrow went down.

At 5:35, Norm entered with Eve on his arm. She was dressed to kill. Again, I thought that this was going to be an interesting evening.

If I had worried about dinner with Eve Hoversal, I needn't have. Within minutes, Michelle and Eve were chatting like old friends. They only stopped when our waitress came over with a complimentary plate of prosciutto and a bowl of olives. She asked if we were ready to order. Norm was about to say something when Michelle asked if she could come back later.

When the waitress left, Michelle and Eve continued talking. By the end of the meal, Norm and I had heard things we never would have learned otherwise. Michelle explained how she had aced out the other three women who had picked me at speed dating. She laughed and told Eve that I hadn't stood a chance. Eve's story was more involved. She'd been married right after college for three years. The last two were spent growing increasingly apart. When the final divorce came through, she decided to punish herself for making such a boneheaded choice of men by not dating for an entire year. Norm came by just before the year was up, and they hit it off immediately. That told me a lot about why Norm had looked like he did on Monday morning.

This wasn't going to be one of those times when we would get in the car and Michelle would say, "What a bitch." I was right.

"I really enjoyed tonight. Norm caught a good one."

"I'm glad for him as well. He was not looking forward to coming back to the city. He only did it as a promise to his father. Maybe now he has another reason."

Eve seemed more real to me than she had in high school. Maybe it was because I had matured and become more confident. I hoped it would end well for Norm.

The mystery as to how Nate the Great would get access to Buddy Doyle once the police had arrested him was soon solved. Nate phoned me at 9 am, shortly after I'd gotten into my car to go to school.

"You're clear to visit Doyle. He signed the paperwork that makes me his lawyer yesterday afternoon. I want you to do the questioning because I don't want him to make the connection between me and Norm's car quite yet."

"Won't he anyway? Isn't it a conflict of interest on your part, representing him and Stemple?"

"No. He's being charged for the shooting at the grocery store, not the hairdresser robbery or Norm's car. The police haven't made those connections, and as far as anyone knows, neither have we. I'm just representing him for the shooting."

"I'll see him this morning. Any suggestions?"

"Start by having him run through the robbery. Look for anything that made him use the gun. Then start asking where he got the gun. See if you can get him to admit he took the files as well, and find out what he did with them."

"Got it." I wanted to ask more, but Nate had hung up.

I shouldn't have been surprised by Nate's solution for getting access to Buddy Doyle. If you had the money, Nate Hart was your guy. What was unusual was for Nate to take a pro bono case. Doyle either didn't know that or didn't care why Nate would offer to help him. The use of a weapon in the grocery store robbery, especially a gun, didn't put the crime one step up; it was elevated several floors.

Buddy Doyle was what I'd expected. Not what he looked like. I already had that image from the pictures we'd recovered, but the rest. The pictures didn't show the neck tats, or those on his knuckles, nor the attitude. He was one hundred percent street punk, and after a few minutes of talking to him, I realized he wasn't too bright either.

"So you're Hart's guy, the PI?" asked Doyle, after he was shackled to the table and the sheriff had left.

"Nate wanted you to know that I'll be asking you questions, and you have to answer them truthfully. It will determine whether he can get you off or at least get the charges reduced."

"Yeah, he told me. What do you want to know?"

"First, tell me everything you did from the time you entered the store until you left."

Doyle went over his actions, basically following what I'd seen on the security footage.

"Okay, why did you pick that store?"

"I went in the week before and bought a soda. He'd jacked up the price by fifty cents on a can of Coke. $3.75 for a Coke. What an asshole."

"Did you have a car?" I asked.

"I was using one I'd borrowed."

I was sure the owner hadn't known he'd lent his car to Doyle.

"Tell me about the gun. Do you always use a gun?"

"Nah. This was the first time. I wish I hadn't brought it. I thought the Chinaman was reaching for one under the counter."

"That's good," I said. "Nate can use that. You thought you were in danger. Where did you get the gun?"

"I found it," said Doyle, looking at his shackled hands.

"Remember what Nate said about telling me the truth. The gun's history is important, real important. If it's been used in other crimes, his whole strategy for getting you off goes out the window."

"I got it from a car I broke into," said Doyle, almost in a whisper.

"That's better. How long ago, and where was it parked?"

"Just a few days ago. Down south of Market. I think it was Mission Street."

"Good. Was it loaded when you found it?"

"Yeah."

"Had you shot it before the robbery? Did you load the bullets?"

"Nah, I used it the way I found it. I did play with it a little. It has a safety switch."

"That's good too," I said. "It proves you're a first-time user. Your fingerprints won't be on the bullets or the casings." I knew that the next few questions were really what Nate was interested in. "Did you take anything else from the car?"

Doyle hesitated. It was obvious he didn't want to say anything. I just stared at him, my pen poised above my legal pad where I'd been writing notes. Finally he looked up.

"Some papers."

"Do you still have them? They might be important in learning whether the owner had a criminal record."

"No. I gave them to a guy. He was the one who hired me to rob the car."

"Even better. Does this guy have a name? How do you know him?"

"He's just a guy from the old days. We belonged to a gang together. His name is Buzz."

"Buzz. What's his last name?"

"Just Buzz. In the gang we only used first names. We thought it was cool that no one could rat on anyone else."

"How do you get in touch with Buzz?"

"I don't. He calls me."

"This is really good information, Buddy. I think Nate will be pleased. He will have more questions, and he'll be with you at your arraignment hearing. That will probably be tomorrow."

I felt that he was telling the truth. I didn't know exactly what Nate would do with the information, but I'd gotten what we wanted. We were getting closer. The more we found out, the more I believed that Stewart Stemple might be innocent. I looked at my watch, folded the legal pad, and rang to be let out.

At the front desk, I asked the sergeant if I could see Stewart Stemple now. He looked annoyed. It was still inside normal visiting hours, but later than usual. The sheriffs for the most part had little love for defense attorneys or their investigators. I stood there while he recited how much time was left and the prisoners' lunch hours, as if a bologna sandwich took an hour to prepare. Finally he ordered that Stemple be brought to interview room #2. I asked the sheriff who escorted me to wait. I wouldn't take long. I only had one question.

"Do you know anyone called Buzz?" I asked, almost before the guard had left the room.

"Buzz? No. Who's Buzz?" asked Stemple.

"He might be a gang member turned legit. He might be the key to a Get Out of Jail Free card for you," I said.

"I never heard of him. When am I going to see Nate? Does he know that I've never even fired a gun?" he asked, working himself up. In his situation, I couldn't blame him.

"Soon," I answered, not knowing if it was true. I got up and rang the buzzer to be let out.

CHAPTER 22

Norm was still in his cramped office, working on his computer, when I got back from the jail.

"How'd it go with Buddy Doyle?" he asked

"Good. Real good. He admitted to robbing your car and taking the gun and the file. Didn't even change the bullets. He gave the files to a guy named Buzz, a friend from the old days."

"Buzz who?"

"No last name. A guy from a gang he belonged to when he was a teenager."

"Nate should get Buddy's rap sheet," said Norm. "Maybe it will give us a chance to get to know Buzz better."

"Great idea. Something Stemple said today bothered me driving back here," I said, taking a seat across from Norm.

"You saw Buddy and Stemple? You've had a busy morning."

"Stemple said he hasn't ever fired a gun. That he wouldn't know how to use one. It made me think of something I learned in PI training."

"What was that?" asked Norm, striking a few keys and closing his computer.

"I remember that the first shot someone takes is the most accurate, due to the gun's recoil."

"I know my gun had a kick. I can't imagine it being less for an Uzi."

"Okay. So in the first office, the murderer enters. The first shot, his most accurate, hits a woman in the leg, and then he nails Fisher with three closely placed taps to his chest. Then in the second office, he fires twice at the woman, one at her head and one at her heart. Both shots would have been fatal. With a bullet left, he doesn't shoot at Stemple. Why treat the two women differently? Why didn't he just wound Madison? It certainly appears the guy is a good shot. It's something Nate should think about. It makes me wonder whether Madison Francis was the killer's primary target in the second office."

"Hmmm," said Norm. "It's worth looking at, since no other lines of questioning seem to be bearing fruit, other than Buddy Doyle. I'd rather you ask Nate about getting his rap sheet."

"I understand. Will do." I got up and went to my office, where D'Jarl was waiting for me.

"Let me make a phone call first," I said to D'Jarl, seeing the look on his face, which told me he had something serious to discuss. I phoned Nate but got his assistant, Linda, instead. Nate was in court.

"Would you please ask Nate to get Buddy Doyle's previous arrest record? I'm particularly interested in a gang he was in as a minor."

Linda said that he was not expected back until after 4:30 or maybe not until morning, if he'd won the case he was working on. I knew that if he won, he'd be having drinks at the Iron Horse, his usual watering hole after a win. Tomorrow would be fine. Buddy wasn't going anywhere and neither were his records.

"How's the case going?" asked D'Jarl as I hung up.

"Not as fast as I'd like. It would be better if Mike Ronning were here, but we might have just caught a break. What's up?"

"This is just between us, all right?"

"Sure." Now I was worried.

"Remember two years ago, when our players who were taking business classes kept complaining about the Chinese guys in the classes?"

"Yeah. They couldn't speak English and were slowing the class down."

"And remember," said D'Jarl, "when our guys complained, Admissions said that they'd all passed the TOEFL test well above the minimum."

"We suggested that they should be retested and put into English second language classes if they didn't pass. Nothing was done, but it caused a stink between Athletics and Admissions—not a good thing."

"That's not exactly true," said D'Jarl. "Nothing was done to that bunch, but a provision was put into the application that included the TOEFL test in the same category as grades, SAT, and prerequisite courses. Any falsification could mean expulsion from school."

"So?"

"So don't you think it's a little strange that Simu passed with a 97 a week after he visited us?"

"He spoke English a lot better than those others," I said, seeing D'Jarl's point. "You think it's something to worry about?"

"I think he better study hard. It would be good if there was no question about his English ability when he enrolled."

"It's on my list to call the coach and ask him what games he plans to attend on our European trip. That might just come up." Simu had taken the TOEFL test in Paris. I didn't know the security measures that were taken to establish identity, but it was possible that another tall Serbian man could have taken the test for Simu. We were one of the few schools that paid a lot of attention to the TOEFL score, and that went double when it came to athletes.

D'Jarl stood, clapped me on the back, and left. Just another thing to worry about.

Madison Francis had lived with a roommate in a small two-bed-room apartment on Beach Street, a block from the Palace of Fine Arts in the Marina district. I didn't expect the roommate to be home, but D'Jarl's suspicion that Simu Vuksan's test score might be in question had unnerved me. I wanted to get away from school and think about something I had control over.

It was a short drive, less than ten minutes. Finding a park-ing spot took five. There was parking at the lake that fronted the Palace, but you had about a three-minute window before your car was broken into. This area, along with Fisherman's Wharf and Ghirardelli Square, were three of the hot spots in San Francisco. I was lucky: I saw a car pulling out on Broderick Street, did a quick three-point turn, and took the spot for myself.

I didn't have Madison's roommate's name or any other infor-mation about her. I'd thought I'd leave a note to call me and my business card. But I didn't have to. She was home and answered the intercom. I explained who I was and that I was an investigator working on Madison's murder. She was cautious. She said to wait and she would be down.

A woman's face appeared in the foot-to-ceiling glass window to the left of the door. It was protected by a wrought-iron barrier.

"ID?"

I caught the words through what must have been double-paned glass. I took out my badge and held it in front of the glass. The door to the building opened, and a tall good-looking redhead stepped out.

"I'm Rob MacKay," I said, showing my badge. "Are you Madison's roommate?"

"Could I see your identification?" she asked, still hesitant.

I took my PI license out of my wallet and handed it to her along with my card.

She took the license, read it, turned it over, and extended her hand. "Sandy Harper. I heard about Madison during our lay-over in New York. I'm a little spooked."

"I can't blame you. I don't think you are in danger, though." I gave her my most reassuring smile. "Would you be able to answer a few questions?"

She seemed to hesitate, looking at me, then said, "Sure. Would you mind if we went to a delicatessen? I was just leaving to get some breakfast."

"That would be fine," I said, thinking that it was after lunch-time. She must have an active nightlife.

Sandy Harper started walking. She walked fast. I noticed she was wearing low-heeled shoes that looked comfortable. Six blocks later, we entered a deli on Chestnut Street. Six blocks, half a mile. I was glad I was in good shape, because Sandy definitely was.

We ordered and sat down, waiting for our number to be called.

"I'm a flight attendant for United. We just got in this morning at ten," Sandy explained.

"Have the police questioned you about Madison yet?"

"No. There are several messages on our home phone, but I've been flying for the last four days. I was going to call them back after breakfast. It's just terrible about Madison." She was starting to tear up.

"How long have you been roommates?"

"Almost two years now. She had the apartment for almost five years. I answered her ad for a roommate. It's been good for both of us. We both respect the apartment and don't get in each other's way."

"Did you know any of her boyfriends?"

"Some. I thought she was killed at work along with a bunch of other people," said Sandy, with a questioning look.

"Only two were killed. Madison and a lawyer on another floor. Did she ever date her boss, Stewart Stemple?"

"No. He would come over occasionally for dinner, but they never dated. He was a nice guy. Madison liked him, but not as a boyfriend. He hit on me, though, so I'm pretty sure he isn't gay."

"How about any other boyfriends?"

"I saw a few when they would pick her up and sometimes sleep over. She was picky. She was starting to look for something stable."

"Can you recall any names?"

"Not really, but she has a desk calendar that has names and notes, dates and places."

"That could be important," I said. "Could I see it, or better yet, borrow it for a day or so?"

"Sure, if it would help catch her killer. Won't the police want it as well, though?"

"Absolutely. Tell you what. I'll take pictures of it. You phone the police and ask for Inspector Farley. I'll give you his direct number. Give him my name and tell him about the calendar. I'm sure he'll be interested."

"I was surprised when I got home," said Sandy, "and found that nobody had been there. I'm sure the police could have gotten some sort of permission, a warrant or something."

Our number was called. "Just a second." I got up and paid for our food, bringing it back to the table.

"The police have made an arrest," I said, putting our food down and taking my chair. "They are sure they have their man. They believe that Madison and the other woman who was shot were just in the wrong place at the wrong time."

"There was another woman shot?"

"Yes, she was on the other floor. She was injured and is recovering. I suspect that seeing Madison's apartment is not a high priority for the police."

"Who did they arrest?"

I was hesitant to tell her after her previous remarks about Stemple, but I knew that it was a must if I was to keep her trust.

"They've arrested Stewart Stemple."

"That's crazy," said Sandy. "He really liked Madison. Heck, I would have dated him if he wasn't her boss."

She asked a few more questions about how Madison had died, finally realizing that I was unwilling to talk about it.

"Would you mind if I got some dessert?" she asked, looking at my half-finished sandwich.

"Not at all." I gave her the smile again. She was easy to smile at.

Sandy came back to the table with the largest slice of chocolate cake I'd ever seen. I didn't know how she kept in shape, but it wasn't from restricting her caloric intake. We talked mostly about life as a flight attendant and how the uneven hours took a toll. I mentioned that I was similarly torn, being an Investigator as well as a basketball coach. Several times I saw Sandy looking at my left hand, where there was no ring. I suspected she might be looking for something a little more stable as well.

"Let me walk you home," I said as she pushed the last crumbs of her cake into the tongs of her plastic fork.

I guess I'd gained her trust, because when we arrived, she invited me up to the fifth floor apartment and showed me Madison's desk and day planner. I took pictures of each page on my phone, then gave her Farley's number. I didn't want her to call him until I'd finished taking my pictures. I asked for my card back and wrote my cell number on the back. I got her cell as well, which she copied onto my phone, giving a hundred-watt smile of her own and a cute cock of the head.

"If you can think of anything, or anyone who might have a grudge against Madison, please call me," I said. I thanked her and left. It felt like I had taken a step forward but didn't know in what direction. I knew it was still a long shot that Madison had been the target. I was growing more certain that Stemple wasn't the shooter.

CHAPTER 23

Leroy "Buzz" Boland was sometimes confused as to which of his identities he was occupying. It had been eighteen years since he had acquired the alternate persona. That had been half his life. For the first ten years, Leroy had provided the means for both his identities to go to college and live. In the last eight, more and more, it had been his real life that had taken over, leaving Leroy not exactly redundant, but at least not needed as much. Fisher's death and the framing of Steward Stemple might be the last things Leroy would have to do.

It had started when his father nicknamed him Buzz. His parents told him that he had crawled at seven months and walked at eleven, both at a furiously fast pace. There wasn't a lamp or a table top that was safe from his ramblings. Fortunately, his mother didn't like the name, and it fell into disuse after his father died of a heart attack when he was twelve.

His mother spent most of her time working or trying to find another man. Having a teenaged son around wasn't helping matters. He was pretty much left alone. That was, until he joined the South of Market Gang when he was fifteen. They thought they were big time and only used first names. He gave them Buzz. They did snatch-and-runs from stores, but as they entered their late teens, they became more ambitious. His last job with the gang was just after he turned 18. It was summer, and one of the older gang members had taken a job with a home security firm, doing electric wiring. One of the families that used the service was going on vacation to Italy for two weeks. He was able to obtain the security code and the address without anyone catching him. The house was in a rich section of Millbrae, just south of San Francisco.

The gang had not only become more ambitious, it had gotten more sophisticated in the three years since he'd joined. They sent one member to the front door with a package. He entered the alarm code, went into the house, then let the others in the back door. While the others looted the downstairs of TVs and silverware, Buzz went upstairs with another guy and went through the bedrooms. They found a jewelry box with a lot of bling hidden deep in a drawer filled with ladies' panties. His partner went downstairs to show his find, while Buzz continued searching. All the loot was to be divided equally. In the man's closet on the top shelf, behind a carefully concealed sliding partition, Buzz found what was probably the reason for the family's wealth. There was a box containing a stack of hundreds almost an inch high, and on quick count, over a thousand 20-milligram Oxycodone tablets in one hundred tablet plastic bottles. Making sure no one was watching, Buzz stuck the money down the front of his pants. The Oxycodone he placed in the front pocket of his hoodie. It made a bulge, which he hid by picking up a small portable TV and holding it in front of him. The TV he would share, the rest he would not.

The gang had finished ransacking the house when he went downstairs. They had come up with a plan that would protect the guy who had stolen the security code. They loaded all the loot into the trunk of the family's SUV and waited while the guy reset the alarm, then opened the front door. The alarm sounded as he ran to the car, joining the rest of the gang. They opened the garage door and drove off with the family's valuables in the homeowner's vehicle. They had left their own cars parked several blocks away in a secluded area. They unloaded the loot, parked the stolen car, and took off. Buzz had passed the TV he was carrying to one of the others, taking nothing, trusting the others to live by the gang's code of sharing.

Once home, he counted the money. $13,300, all in crisp hundreds. He didn't use drugs or sell them, but he estimated the value of the drugs was between $15 and $25 dollars a tab. One thing was for sure, he was going to need more than just the false identity of "Buzz" if he was going to get rid of the stuff without leaving a trail. Buzz suspected that most of the gang would end up in jail, not for this heist, but surely in the future. He was smart. He had already received word that he'd been admitted to the University of California. It wasn't his first choice. It had been UCLA. He wanted out of San Francisco. He had another life planned–two lives, actually.

He'd heard of a Mexican man named Angel who was supplying papers for illegals. He was supposed to be good, but expensive for those who needed his help. It was a piece of information he'd stashed away as unimportant, until now. It took a while to find the guy's number. It was answered on the third ring. Buzz said he'd heard that Angel was an artist and wanted to talk to him about a couple pieces of his art. Angel sounded suspicious; Buzz didn't have an accent, not his usual client. He finally agreed to meet in Mission Dolores Park the next day at noon. The artist would bring a few pieces that Buzz could look at.

The next day, Buzz went to the park early. It was one of those glorious days when the fog had retreated early, leaving the houses looking like they had been freshly painted. People had already staked out their personal spaces on the grass with beach towels, folding aluminum chairs, and lounges. In the center of the grass was a small dark-haired man standing in front of an easel. The artist was early as well. Buzz watched him for ten minutes before moving casually toward him. Approaching, he took in the man's features. Obviously Latino, he was beardless, with a pointed jaw and straight nose. His mouth was wide and curved up a little at the ends. His eyes were sharp, dark, and focused on the painting in front of him. Buzz moved past him, then turned, as if to see what the artist was painting. Resting against the easel were two other paintings. The picture he was working on was of the Mission Dolores but not of the Basilica. It was centered on the graveyard and the garden just to the south. The old Mission wall took up the right side of the canvas, casting a reflective light on the central painting showing the paths through red roses and a statue of a priest with a downcast head in the background. The painting was both sad and happy at the same time.

Buzz remarked that it was a wonderful painting and asked if the rest of his work was as good. The man answered that it was probably better, and asked if he was Buzz.

"I am, and you are Angel?" asked Buzz, knowing the answer.

The man put down his brush, picked up one of the works leaning against the easel, and turned it toward Buzz. He asked Buzz if he liked it.

"I'm looking for something much smaller, but just as excellent in quality," said Buzz. Angel smiled and said that he was very young to appreciate good art. Buzz could tell the man was still suspicious.

Buzz knew he had to convince the artist that he was not a cop if there was ever to be an understanding between them.

"I'm not a cop," he said, unbuckling his jeans and dropping his pants to his thighs. He was going commando. Showing himself was something no cop would ever do. Angel smiled, lifted a thumb on his right hand as if measuring Buzz's manhood for a painting, and said that he would consider the type of art he wanted for a hundred dollars. If he declined to do the work, the hundred wouldn't be refunded. If he decided to take Buzz on as a customer, they would agree to a price, but his better work would cost several thousand dollars. Buzz agreed, gave the man a hundred, his cell phone number, and a list of items, admired the painting for another minute, and left the park. He suspected that Angel would have him followed, and he was right. As Buzz drove off, he noticed a Latino boy jotting down his license plate number.

The phone call came early the next afternoon. Angel gave him his address, which was near Sanchez and Jersey Street. He was told to bring the money. The house looked like any non-descript two-story that had been built between the Victorian era and the modern duplexes that now dominated the area. Buzz rang the bell and was let in by Angel, who led him down a flight of stairs to what must originally have been the garage. Angel asked him exactly what he wanted the items on the list for. Buzz said a whole new identity. Angel looked at him. It was a strange request for one so young. They usually just wanted an ID that would let them buy liquor.

"Do you really need a new identity?" asked Angel. "Or just enough of one to allow you to buy booze?"

Buzz knew what he wanted, and it had nothing to do with buying liquor. He said that he wanted a complete identity, one that he could live with indefinitely. Angel looked at him for a long time before agreeing. He had Buzz put on a shirt and tie and stand against a blue backdrop. He took several pictures, full frontal and profile. He also took impressions of Buzz's fingertips in some sort of wet goo, which he explained was an alginate. He poured some plastic into the goo after it had set, gave Buzz a towel to wipe his hands clean, and took him back upstairs.

"What you ask for will cost $5,000," said Angel, as they stood by the front door. "Are you prepared to spend that much?" Buzz said that he was, and asked how long it would take.

"I'll have the necessary documents for you next week," answered Angel, stressing that his instructions would be as important as the ID.

The week-long wait was hard for Buzz. He worried that someone in the gang would discover that he'd held out on them. He needed to make a complete break, and he needed to do it quickly. He worried that the homeowner would come back and discover the theft, and the police would figure out that the gang had done it. He was relieved when he got Angel's phone call to come to his house the next day for the painting.

At 10 am, Buzz rang the doorbell. The kid he'd seen taking his license plate number opened the door and led him downstairs. Angel was working with his back to him on what looked like an overhead projector. Without turning, he asked if Buzz had the money. Buzz said he did and pulled out the $5,000. The kid took it and spread it out on a table, shining a colored light on it. Satisfied it was real, he counted it, then took it to Angel, telling him in Spanish that it was all there. Finally Angel turned around, greeting Buzz with a smile. He had Buzz sit at the table where the kid had counted the money and sat across from him.

"You're lucky, I found an identity that will fit and will pass any scrutiny." He explained to Buzz that his new name was Leroy Boland and that he'd been born in Van Nuys, California. The real Leroy had died at 14 years old, looking left instead of right on a London street.

"His father worked for the Ford Motor company in Sweden. He was visiting the Aston Martin plant and had taken his son. The boy's death has not been reported in the States."

Angel had some photographs of the boy. Buzz could pass for an older version of the kid if no one looked closely. He gave Buzz a birth certificate and two credit cards, a San Francisco library card, and a picture ID from San Francisco State College. Last was a Wells Fargo checking account with two hundred dollars in it. It was less than Buzz had expected. Angel explained that the credit cards were real and could be used, and the same was true of the checking account. The Chase card was from Costco and had his picture on it. He would just have to give them a new address as soon as possible. The birth certificate was also real. He could get anything with it, including a passport, should he want it. The real Leroy Boland's had just expired. He suggested that Buzz get a California driver's license on his own. He had the kid bring him a small plastic case that held what looked like a number of large contact lenses. He explained that these were fingerprints for both Buzz's right and left thumbs. He showed Buzz how to apply them and take them off without damaging them.

"Use them when you get the license," he explained. "Once you have that as an ID, you can get almost anything."

Angel answered questions for ten minutes, then handed Buzz a small canvas wrapped in paper. "I hope you like your purchase," he said, and turned back to his work on the overhead projector. The kid took Buzz to the front door and let him out.

Buzz got in his car and drove across the Golden Gate Bridge to San Rafael. He put the first and last month's rent and the security deposit down on a small apartment in his new name. With time still left, he drove to the Department of Motor Vehicles in

Corte Madera and made an appointment to take a driver's test for a license. Then he went to the AT&T store in Mill Valley to get Leroy Boland a phone. Tomorrow he would get a P.O. box for Boland and one for himself. Then Leroy would apply for admission to the College of Marin.

CHAPTER 24

I used the school's printer to copy the pages of Madison Francis's day planner from my phone. I made two copies, one to share with Norm and one to give to Nate. I wished I had Madison's phone so I that I'd have the contact numbers that corresponded to the dates. Even if the police thought Madison was collateral damage, they weren't likely to part with that.

Norm was at his desk, looking bored. I flipped him the first four months of one of the set of copies. I kept the latter four months of May, June, July, and August.

"Madison Francis's date calendar," I said in response to his look.

That perked him up. "How did you get this?"

"You forget how charming I am. Her roommate let me see it. She's a looker if Eve doesn't work out," I said, giving him a punch on the shoulder.

"Yeah, right."

Both of us started going through the pages, Norm from January on and me from August back. Madison's handwriting was elegant but hard to read, tight and small, sometimes filling the entire square for the date. We had been at it for almost half an hour when I shouted, "Got it!"

Norm followed with, "Me too!"

There it was, on May eleventh. *Mill Valley Music Festival-Buzz.* Scratched over it in large print was *JERK.* It was hard to tell on the copy, but it looked as if *JERK* had almost penetrated the original page. Norm had found two earlier entries on April 20th and 27th. *Buzz dinner* and *Buzz dinner and show.*

It was time to talk to Sandy Harper again. I hoped I wouldn't wake her up, after what she had told me of her irregular hours after European flights. My bigger worry was that she might already have talked with Inspector Farley and that he'd told her not to talk to me again.

"Hi, Sandy. It's Rob MacKay."

If Farley had discouraged her, it didn't seem to make a difference. Sandy was glad to hear from me. I switched my phone to speaker, putting my finger to my lips for Norm.

"Rob, I'm glad you called."

"I hope I didn't wake you," I said.

"No. I try to stay awake at least until nine on the days I arrive back in San Francisco, unless I'm scheduled to fly out again the next day. Then I go to sleep about now. I'm free all afternoon."

"I wanted to ask you a few questions."

"Sure, like I said, I'm free all afternoon. Just ring the bell and I'll let you in."

"I was hoping to do some of it on the phone," I said. "Do you know anything about a guy named Buzz who Madison might have dated?"

"That asshole?" Sandy seemed really mad at the mention of Buzz. It took me a little by surprise.

"I take it you know him?"

"I met him before their first date, sometime after April 15th. I remember because he was bragging about getting big bucks back from the income tax. He wouldn't have been my choice for a date, but Madison didn't seem to mind his bragging. She said he had a really expensive car."

"I was looking at May 11 on her planner. She had *Mill Valley Music Festival–Buzz*, crossed off with *JERK!* Do you know anything about that?"

"I sure do. It might take a while. Are you sure you don't want to come over?"

"I can't. I have an appointment downtown in an hour. What about Buzz on that date?"

"I was flying when she had her second date with him," she said. "Thank God I was here for the third. They went to an outdoor music festival somewhere in Marin County. They came back here and had a fight. I was in my room. There was always a chance that Madison might let someone spend the night. If that was the case, then I wouldn't come out of my own bedroom, as things might be uncomfortable."

"What was the fight about?"

"As soon as I heard it, I came out. Buzz was yelling, really mad. He was drunk. Madison was trying to explain, but he was just getting angrier. He was shouting she had no business looking at his private papers. She turned away and he grabbed her and spun her around. He pinched both of her nipples. She screamed. I called 911 and yelled that I had called the police, which seemed to have an immediate effect. He yelled 'Bitch!' and ran out of the apartment. That's the last we saw of him. Madison thought about filing charges. She had big bruises on each of her breasts. I kept after her to contact the police, but she just didn't want to have anything more to do with the guy."

Norm passed me a note. I read it and asked his question. "Do you have any idea what they were fighting about?"

"Not then. But Madison and I talked about it later. He'd had a number of beers at the festival. Enough that Madison said that she should drive. He wouldn't have it and stopped at a liquor store on the way home. He evidently had a tough time choosing a bottle of wine and some vodka. I still have them here if you want them. They're still in the bag."

"I do want them," I said. "Could I send someone over to get them?"

"Oh." She sounded disappointed.

"I'll send my best friend. His name is Norm. He's a lot nicer than I am. Besides the drinking, what were they fighting about?"

"While Buzz was in the liquor store, Madison was looking for some lotion. They'd been in the sun all day. She opened his glove box. There was no lotion, but she read the car's registration. Like I said, it was a BMW, one of the real expensive models. It was registered to someone else. There was also a wallet with a driver's license that had someone else's name on it but Buzz's picture. She closed the glove box, but when they got home, she asked him about it. That's when he started yelling about his personal papers."

"Sandy, this is great. It is very important that you don't touch the wine or vodka bottles. Norm will also want to take your fingerprints so they can be excluded from Buzz's. We already have Madison's. I'll phone you as soon as I get through with my meeting and we'll arrange to talk again. Please give Norm your work schedule? You're the best."

"You coward," said Norm, as I hung up and wrote down Madison and Sandy's address. "I have a meeting downtown. Give me a break. I'm supposed to believe that she's good-looking?"

"Swear to it. Someone has to get this information to Nate. I knew which of the two you'd prefer to visit." I gave him a glass. "Wipe that clean and have her put both hands on it, including her thumbs. That will give us her fingerprints. Be careful with the bottles. Don't take them out of the bag and don't touch them. If you can use a pair of kitchen tongs, all the better. We might get some prints from the bag as well."

Norm left and I phoned Nate's office. He wasn't in or taking calls, but would return at 4 pm. I made an appointment and settled down to study what I had learned. I tried to anticipate what Nate would ask, and I realized I'd made a big mistake. I quickly called Sandy Harper again.

"Sandy. It's Rob again. Sorry to bother you, but I forgot to ask if you knew Buzz's full name?"

"Yes, but he never used it. Madison and I used to kid about it. If I were named Leroy, I would use my nickname as well."

"His name is Leroy? Do you have a last name?"

"Brown," said Sandy. "Wait, that's just what we joked about. Big, bad Leroy Brown. It started with a B, though. I just can't think of it right now."

"Norm will be over in a few minutes to pick up the bottles. If you think of it, tell him. It's very important."

"Will do."

I thanked her and hung up. Leroy "Buzz" B….. It was something to go on, but it would be a lot better to have the last name.

I had half an hour to waste before driving downtown. I put on my gym shoes and went down to the Malloy court. I started shooting free throws, using the repetition to relax myself. I was at it for ten minutes when Booker Oowaite came in and joined me. By rule I wasn't supposed to coach the freshman yet, but after watching me sink twelve straight, Booker asked me to help him with his free throw technique. Like most big men, Booker had big hands. It was their position on the ball that was the key to good shot-making. I showed him how to cradle the ball in his fingertips, the correct posture and stance, all of what D'Jarl had taught me was correct for a big man shooting from the line. Being tall, they often had a flatter trajectory for their free throw attempts. At least what I taught him wouldn't be at odds with what D'Jarl would tell him when practice began in less than a week. I almost lost track of the time, and had to run up to my office and get my wallet and keys. I drove down to Nate's in my gym shoes.

I was surprised to see Norm sitting in Nate's waiting room, a bag with the top of two bottles showing sitting beside him. Between his legs was a blue and white Chinese vase about 18 inches in height.

"You could have told me she was a redhead," he said by way of greeting.

"Would it have made a difference?" I laughed.

"You know how I feel about redheads."

I didn't, but I suspected it was all right because of the grin on his face. I was about to ask him about it when Nate rushed in and waved us into his office.

"Good to see you both," said Nate, much more pleasantly than when I was alone and without Norm. "I take it you have something good to tell me."

"It starts with Buddy Doyle. He gave us the name Buzz. On a hunch, I went over to Madison Francis's apartment and caught her roommate as she was coming out for lunch. She told me that Madison had a desk calendar that had names, dates, and places on it. I was able to take pictures of it."

"Why were you so interested in her?" asked Nate.

"I've always thought it was odd that she was shot three times, any one of them fatal, while Kirsten Grant was just injured. Anyway, there it was on her calendar–Buzz, three times, the last one scratched out with *JERK*."

That caught Nate's attention. I motioned for Norm to tell him the rest.

Norm went over the fight, the car registration, the second wallet, and the two bottles of booze.

"What's with the vase?" I asked Norm.

"Sandy, that's the roommate, remembered some things after you questioned her, or maybe she just liked me better. She remembered that on the first date, Buzz had picked up the vase and asked how expensive it was. She said they should have known right then that he was an asshole. I thought if there were prints on the vase, we could differentiate them from those of the liquor store clerk."

"Good thinking," said Nate. "Did you get a name to go with Buzz?"

"Kind of," I said. "Leroy Brown."

"Leroy Boland," said Norm, smiling. "I told you she liked me better. Oh, I might have slipped and told Sandy that you were getting married in a month."

"Have you got a line on this Leroy Boland?" asked Nate, ignoring the look I gave Norm.

"No, we just got this information less than an hour ago. We wanted to get the prints to you before the police find out what we've done."

"All right," said Nate. He picked up his cell phone and hit an automatic dial. When it was answered, Nate said that he had something to be fingerprinted and to bring two large evidence bags.

"Where is the day planner?" he asked as soon as he'd disconnected.

"The roommate thought the police would want it after I took pictures. I've emailed the shots to you already."

"I can't understand why the police haven't gotten this already," said Nate.

"Sandy, the roommate, is a flight attendant," said Norm. "She's been in Europe for the last four or five days. We lucked out."

"Good work," said Nate. "Find out as much as you can about Leroy Boland. Try to find out what that extra wallet is about. We have a direct link from your file being stolen to Buddy Doyle to this Buzz. It might not stop there. Oh, and Norm, hands off the flight attendant until the case is over. It's just the kind of thing that could ruin the evidence you brought me."

Norm frowned. I would have to ask him what I couldn't remember about how he felt about redheads.

"Do you want me to ask Buddy Doyle anything more about Leroy Boland?" I asked Nate.

"No. Don't go near him. He's no longer my client."

"How…?" I stuttered.

"After what you got from him, we didn't need anymore. I gave a release paper to the judge at his arraignment, citing conflict of interest. Of course, I didn't know there was one until you interviewed him. The judge will rule on it soon. Let Doyle find a public defender." Nate smiled. "This new information changes everything. Stemple was in jail when your car was broken into. We just have to find out if there's a connection between him and Leroy Boland."

"Your dad's a piece of work," I said to Norm as we rode down in the elevator.

"Yeah. That Buddy Doyle bit is borderline illegal. He'll get away with it because, except for the picture near my car, there was no real evidence that Doyle did the break-in, and he was only representing the guy for the grocery store shooting."

"Like I said, a piece of work." To change subjects, I asked Norm, "Would you like to take a short walk and see Michelle's new digs? It's just a few blocks away and I haven't seen them yet."

"Sure. Should we take a car?"

"Nah, let's leave them here. You dad can pay the parking."

CHAPTER 25

I gave Michelle a call as Norm and I walked the six blocks to her office. The light to cross Market Street seemed to take as long as it took to walk the half-mile. It was the first time I'd been to the new space. The last time I went to the Foundation, it was located in Santa Clara. Then, I'd been investigating the previous director's disappearance and interviewing the staff along with Captain Wu of the Woodside police.

Not only was there security at the entrance fronting Second Street, but the door to the Dorrinson Foundation on the eighth floor looked solid and locked. I noticed a camera behind glass in a small niche above the door. Michelle had told me that the staff was worried about security, so she had hired a firm when putting the office together. The buzzer to the side of the door emitted a pleasant chime. I was wondering if the staff knew that Michelle was my fiancée, after knowing me only as the PI who helped catch their former boss's murderer. I shouldn't have worried. As I entered with Norm at my back, they stood and clapped. Michelle had obviously paved the way.

"Close up what you're working on. We stop early today," said Michelle. "I think you know my fiancé, Rob, and this is his friend, Norm Hart."

Most of them closed their computer screens with a rapid series of clicks and came around the desk to where Norm and I stood. I particularly remembered James Armbruster. He was six-three and stooped, and his hair was already thinning. He was the first to come up and shake my hand.

"Mrs. Dorrinson told us what you did for her," he said. "Thank you, and thanks for the suggestion of moving the foundation to San Francisco. It's saved three of us at least a half hour in our commute. Barret is the only one who's longer, and she's looking for an apartment up here."

I had nothing to do with the move north. It had been in the works before I ever started to work for Janet Dorrinson. I kept quiet. I'd let Michelle clear that up if necessary.

I was welcomed by the rest of them in turn. Barret Sorrenson was last. She was the one who'd been so down on Bret Armanino and happy that Sue Brascco was dating Dr. Leslie, who turned out to be her murderer. I couldn't help but wonder if she had made other bad choices in men.

Norm gave a courtesy handshake to Armbruster and turned his attention to the two women. They couldn't have been less alike. Barret Sorrenson was cute, not more than five-three, with almost a boy's haircut. She was full of energy. The other woman was Mary Lynn Smith, who was also good-looking but in a more regal way. Mary Lynn was at least 5'10" in her heels, with shoulder-length blond hair. When Janet had first talked about finding a new director, I'd thought that Mary Lynn would be her choice.

They all seemed happy, but I couldn't tell if it was because of Michelle, the new office, the shorter commute, or the fact that they had knocked off an hour and a half early.

I saw Michelle whispering to Armbruster, who quietly left the office. The question of where he had gone was answered in less than ten minutes, when he returned with four bottles of wine and some real glass stemware.

"I've been meaning to christen the office, and this seems as good a time as any," said Michelle, handing me the wine to open. I knew that Armbruster was an expert on computers. Now I suspected he knew his wine as well. Two bottles were premium whites, and both reds were Napa Valley cabernets. Michelle discreetly poured my glass from a can of 7-Up, which she took from a refrigerator in a small kitchen area in the back of the new space. The new office had a lounge area with a small table set between a couch and several padded chairs. The room smelled of fresh paint, with light pastels covering adjacent walls. The rug looked expensive and covered the entire space except the kitchen nook.

"I know it's last minute," said Michelle, halfway through her second glass of wine, "but how would everyone like to go to dinner? My treat. Norm, you're invited too."

Everyone thought it was a wonderful idea.

"James, would you see if we can get a table for seven at John's Grill? Say, in half an hour?"

Armbruster pulled out his cell phone like Wyatt Earp, a move I remembered from before. In less than two minutes, the reservation was made and everyone was gathering their things for the trek back across Market Street.

I walked hand in hand with Michelle to John's Grill. The others were in front of us with Armbruster leading the way. I couldn't help but notice that Norm was talking up Barret Sorrenson. It had been quite a day for Norm. Besides helping me with the Stemple investigation, he had hooked up with two additional good-looking women. Not bad for being back in San Francisco for less than a week. As we were waiting for our table, I heard him say to Barret that he knew a woman with a great apartment in the Marina who had recently lost a roommate and might be looking for someone to share it with her. I couldn't imagine how he would handle that situation. If he was planning to date both Sandy Harper and

Barret, that was his problem, not mine. It was as if Norm was two different people, I thought. He was the efficient lawyer when we were working on the case, and the single playboy when he was around women. It got me thinking about the second wallet Sandy Harper had mentioned–the one in the BMW's glove box with Buzz's picture but a different name. How I wished we had that other name.

By the time we were finished, with Michelle picking up the check, the restaurant was filled with a line waiting outside. Our eating so early had been the only way we had gotten a table. Michelle had had a third glass of wine, so I offered to drive her home in my car and take her in the next morning. She smiled, kissed me on the cheek, and thanked me, and we said goodbye to the rest of the group.

"I was wondering if you could help me with something," I said when we were in my car and on the approach to the Golden Gate Bridge.

"What?"

"I know the name of the person who ordered Norm's car broken into. He also dated one of the women who was shot. Would you do a complete search on him? Also, see if you can find a link to another person, perhaps the same guy using a different name. You're so much better at that sort of thing than I am." It was no lie, she was. It was Michelle who had discovered that Dr. Leslie owned a boat berthed at Half Moon Bay, and that there was a surveillance camera that might cover the dock. It led to the arrest of the doctor for the murder of Sue Brascco, Bret Armanino, and Alfred Quine.

"Sure, but not tonight." She placed her hand on my inner thigh and my old Camry jumped forward ten miles per hour faster.

—

D'Jarl came into my office at 9:30 the next morning, looking relieved.

"The last passports are taken care of. Domingo's and Booker's. Funny that the two Native Americans need a passport to get back into the country. I was the only coach who had to renew."

"Mine expired last year but when Michelle and I were getting serious, I renewed it, thinking we might go somewhere together."

"Where are you taking your honeymoon?"

"We decided to wait until March Madness is over. I don't want to leave you and Tip alone. God knows what might happen."

"Yeah, right," said D'Jarl.

"Really. Michelle has her hands full with her new job at the Dorrinson Foundation. She wouldn't feel good about leaving, and neither would I. If we wait until after the season is over, we can take off for a couple of weeks and not feel guilty or worried about having to rush back."

The door opened, and Norm came in without knocking. D'Jarl stood, offering the chair to Norm. "Keep him busy," said D'Jarl as he bumped fists with Norm. "He's been complaining that he has nothing to do."

They both laughed as D'Jarl maneuvered his 6' 11" frame past Norm.

"I looked up Leroy 'Buzz' Boland," said Norm, taking the seat that D'Jarl had left. "Not much to find. Nate got his driver's license, but it's not much help. The picture is at least twenty years old, and his address is for a place in San Rafael. It's a house owned by a senior who rents rooms. I've got a phone number for a land line, but so far no one has answered."

"What does the description say?"

Norm took a copy of the license from his pocket, unfolded it, and gave it to me.

"Five foot eleven. A hundred and seventy-five pounds. Hair, blond. Eyes, brown. Did your dad have anyone run the thumbprint?"

"Yeah, it's clean. But he's the same size as the eye witness gave us."

"So is Stemple. It would have been much better if the gunman had taken off his mask or shouted out his name." I laughed. If he had, I would be out of a job. "It's hard to tell from this black and white copy, but does this guy looks like he's blond? His eyebrows are certainly dark. The last license I got, they didn't look at the information I put down, only the thumbprint. You think this guy could have fudged the description?"

"Let's get a better copy, a color one," said Norm. "I'm sure Nate knows someone who can age it, give us a rendering of what he would look like in his late thirties. I'll get on it. Do you think this is our guy?"

"So far everything is circumstantial. When we get better photos, we can show it around Lester Fisher's office and to Stemple."

I called Nate's office and Nate took the call. I gave Norm most of the credit for what we had. Conversations were always better with Nate when Norm was getting credit or praise. Nate had already ordered the photos, including the aged copy. They would be ready this afternoon.

I'd just hung up when my cell phone buzzed.

"MacKay," said Inspector Farley of the San Francisco Police Department. "Who is Leroy Boland?" I could tell he was pissed.

"Inspector Farley," I said. "I was expecting your call. Have you seen Madison Francis's day planner?"

"Yes, and I understand you took pictures of it and questioned her roommate. You took some things from the apartment that might yield prints?"

"That's true."

"That apartment is a crime scene!"

"I wasn't aware of that. There was no tape, and Sandy Harper, Madison's roommate, didn't seem to know it was either."

"I want the bottles and the vase you took back."

"Inspector, I'm sure you're aware that I'm attorney Nate Hart's investigator and that he's representing Stewart Stemple. We've accounted for the chain of custody for those items. I'm sure that they will be available to you in discovery." Farley was a good police officer. I'd worked with him several times when we were on the same side of the case. I didn't want to anger him, so I kept to myself that he'd certainly had the chance to get the items before me. There was a long silence on the other end.

"The DA will be requesting those immediately," said Farley.

"I'll tell Nate and suggest that he turn them over as soon as they are printed," I said, trying to recover some of the sense of cooperation that Farley and I had had in the past.

"Who is Leroy Boland?" Farley asked again.

"We don't know, other than that he and Madison Francis had a fight." I wasn't about to tell him about Boland's driver's license and that he had hired Buddy Doyle to break into Norm's car.

"Is he involved in her murder?"

"Inspector, if I had proof of that, Nate would know and you would know a few seconds later. We're trying to find out who committed these murders, the same as you. We just don't believe that it was Stewart Stemple. For anything else, I suggest you ask Mr. Hart."

"Well done," said Norm as I disconnected.

I looked at the wall clock. It was almost lunch time.

"You up for Tommy's Joynt?" The answer was obvious. Who wouldn't be, especially with Nate picking up the tab and passing it on to Stemple?

CHAPTER 26

I should have thought of the serving size–that was part of the deal at Tommy's Joynt. I couldn't finish my pastrami with Swiss sandwich, probably because I'd also ordered the potato salad and taken two free pickles from the barrel at the end of checkout. I got a take-home container and put half the sandwich into it, along with a pickle. It was going to be hard staying awake all afternoon. We'd taken Norm's car because he had to move it anyway due to the two-hour parking restriction around the school. At an inner city school, parking was at a premium. Even professors and athletic staff had to pay a stiff fee for the right to park on campus.

Norm found a spot on Roselyn, just half a block from the gym. We had just gotten out of the car when Michelle called my cell.

"We just got back from lunch," I said. "Could I call you back in five?"

"I'll call you," said Michelle and disconnected.

I had a feeling I knew what Michelle's call was about. We went to Norm's office, where there was less chance of being interrupted. Ten minutes after Michelle's first call, my phone chimed.

"Hi, honey. I'm with Norm and you're on speaker."

"That's fine. He'll want to hear this as well. Leroy Boland has a driver's license issued in Corte Madera. It's on its fourth reissue. He no longer lives at the stated address."

"Nate got a copy of it already. The picture on it is from twenty years ago. The thumbprint is clean. No arrests. In fact, we can't find it in any database other than the DMV's."

"That's not surprising," said Michelle. "They might have his prints at the College of Marin. He went there from 1999 through 2001. Got straight A's. Graduated with an AA. He was eligible to enter the UC system as a junior. UC Irvine assigned him a spot but he never enrolled. He has no record of employment, although he does have a Social Security card."

"How did he support himself? He was driving a car worth a hundred and thirty-five thousand. Very interesting."

"Not as interesting as the rest," said Michelle. "He was born in 1981, in Van Nuys. When he was twelve, his father and mother moved to Gothenburg, Sweden to work in Volvo's U.S. division and took Leroy with them. Two years later, in 1996, the boy was struck and killed by a car walking across a street in London. Whoever the present Leroy is, he's stolen the original kid's identity. Evidently the family stayed in Sweden after their son's death and it was never reported stateside."

"Holy shit!" said Norm. "It was bad enough that we had a ghost gun to deal with. Now we have a ghost Leroy."

"There was nothing on Leroy from his death in 1996 until late 1999, when he entered the College of Marin. Then there's a flurry of activity–a reissue of his passport as an adult. He got a driver's license, using a house in San Rafael as his mailing address. Credit cards and a hefty bank account. Just no record of a job."

"You are absolutely amazing," I said. "Would you send this to Nate in an email? I don't want to forget anything when I talk to him."

"Sure," said Michelle. "One more thing, though. There's no record of him owning a car, at least in California. You might ask the roommate if she noticed the license plate–if it was a California plate or from another state."

"So we have someone running around with the identity of a dead man," said Norm after Michelle had hung up. "Someone almost completely off the grid, borrowing an expensive car from someone and dating girls. Sounds like a fun guy."

No sooner had I hung up than Norm's computer dinged with an incoming email.

"All right!" he exclaimed, clicking some keys as the printer started cycling color pages out onto its tray. "These are better." Norm handed me two enhanced pictures of Leroy Boland. One was of the original license shot. The other was an aged version of what Boland might look like now. Both were clear and in color. A note on the bottom said that it appeared that the man in the DMV photo was trying to disguise his looks. It was something I'd thought too when I'd seen the first copy. His eyes were almost closed, his mouth pulled down at the corners with his lips sucked in. I'd never seen a DMV photo that was flattering, but this was the worst. The modern rendition could have been twenty percent of the men who passed you on the street in the financial district at lunch time.

"I'll run this over and show it to Sandy," said Norm. "Is there anything else, besides if she remembers anything about Leroy's car?"

"Ask her about the color of his eyes and hair. It could confirm that he phonied the license description."

"If we're through here, I'll probably take her to dinner after," said Norm with a grin.

"Remember what Nate said. Hands off until the case is finished. Another thing, what about Eve Hoversal?" I was beginning to think that Norm was trying to make up for lost time now that he was back in San Francisco.

"Eve's great, but she's seriously messed up. Probably will be for a year or two. She's coping with her divorce. Right now she's filling her time with guys. I have no reason to think I'll be the only one."

"Okay, I'll see you tomorrow."

After Norm left, I stayed in his office, looking at the picture. Other than Sandy, whom Norm was taking care of, who could I show it to? Stemple, of course. I pulled a yellow pad toward me and started a list, beginning with Stemple, then Randolph Forsythe, Buddy Doyle, Frank Whistel, and perhaps Fisher's receptionist, though that would blow my cover. Norm could show it to her. In fact, as good looking as she was, he'd like the assignment.

I wondered if Nate could get access to the security camera footage in the lobby of 560 Mission. He'd tried the day of the murder, but now it would be part of discovery.

The shooting of Madison Francis still bothered me. Was there any connection between Fisher and Madison Francis? That was something we hadn't considered. She had always been considered collateral damage, much like Kirsten Grant. Now, with the connection to Leroy Boland, it was possible that she was the target.

I called Norm. He was still driving. "Norm, see if Sandy has any pictures of Madison. If she does, get them. I think we should show them around as well as Leroy's."

"Got it," said Norm. "I'm just looking for a parking spot now."

"Don't park at the Palace of Fine Arts," I said. "One set of car windows is enough to have to replace."

I hung up and phoned Nate. He'd received Michelle's email and was excited.

"This guy is the golden egg. It would almost be better if we didn't find him. He's the perfect straw man. With what we have, I would win an acquittal."

"How is that?" I asked, confused.

"What if you find him and he has a perfect alibi?" said Nate. "Still, it's better if we can prove he was the murderer."

"Inspector Farley called me this morning," I said. "He wants the bottles and the vase."

"I bet," said Nate with a chuckle.

"He also asked who Leroy Boland was. I told him he was a guy who had a fight with Madison. I forgot to mention the car break-in and the stolen file, or the connection to the car break-in and the haircut. When will you get the prints off the stuff?"

"They're done. Something strange, though. We got prints that match off the bottles and the vase, enough to differentiate them from the liquor store clerk, whose prints are only on the bottles."

"What's strange about them?"

"The thumbprint doesn't match his license," said Nate.

"That is strange. How many layers of deception does this guy have?" I finished by telling Nate what Norm and I were going to do with the pictures. He approved. I asked if he would call Farley and volunteer the wine bottles and the vase. They would have to be turned over in discovery anyway, and it might salvage a little in my relationship with Farley.

"Will do. This is our guy," said Nate. "Find him before the police do." The line went dead.

I'd almost forgotten that one of the great benefits Michelle had in working for the Dorrinson Foundation and moving to San Francisco was better hours. It hadn't worked that way for the first several weeks, while she was overseeing the move north, but that was now done. She was in the kitchen preparing our dinner as I opened the door.

"It smells great," I said, coming up behind her and kissing her neck. There was rice cooking slowly on one side of the stove and a white sauce with peas and some sort of cubed meat on another burner. A salad bowl was already on the table.

"I thought we'd try something new," said Michelle, turning and giving me a kiss, being careful to keep the wooden spoon she was holding away from my back.

This time I was the one who went to the bathroom and washed up. When I came back, Michelle was spooning the meat sauce onto a bed of rice. There was already an NA beer poured for me and a glass of wine for her.

"Nate really liked the work you did on Leroy Boland," I said as I sat down and spread a napkin on my lap. "He's sure that if it went to trial tomorrow, he'd win an acquittal."

"That's fine," said Michelle, sliding into the seat across from me. "But we both know the trial won't be tomorrow. More likely it will be lucky to start in three months."

"Let's not talk about it now. What is in this fantastic concoction?"

"It's a recipe that I saw in the Sunday paper. Chicken with capers in white sauce. Do you like it?"

"Fantastic, don't throw away that recipe."

"I won't. I did something else today as well. I hired a carpenter to build an arbor for our wedding. I looked at the one the Meadow Club has and I wanted something more substantial. He's going to show us a couple designs. He'll construct it, bring it to the club, dismantle it, and bring it to our backyard."

"My, you have been busy."

—

After I cleaned up the dishes and saved the rest of the sauce, we sat down in the front room and I told Michelle all that had happened that day. I showed her the photographs.

"It's like he's trying to look ugly," said Michelle as she studied Leroy's license photograph.

"That's what Nate's video guy said. It made the modern likeness harder to predict."

We agreed that we had talked enough about work and settled down to watch an episode of *Ted Lasso*.

CHAPTER 27

I entered the school, passing by the Malloy practice gym. Hearing the sound of balls bouncing, I looked in. It was only 9:30 in the morning, but there were seven players shooting free throws. Avery Pierson was under one of the baskets working with Booker Oowaite, while D'Andre Blaston was looking on and asking questions. I wasn't supposed to watch them practice for another two days, ten days before we left for Spain. Time was getting short.

Norm was in his office. He looked spent. There were dark circles under his eyes and his hair was matted on one side. I immediately thought of Nate's warning about staying away from Sandy Harper. I'd thought that Norm was smarter than that.

"Don't tell me? Your dinner date got a little complicated?" I asked.

"Oh it did, but not with Sandy if that's what you're worrying about," said Norm. "Sandy got called in from stand-by. She was flying out at 8:30. She'll only be gone a day and a half, though. I'll pick her up when she returns. Turns out Eve was free for the evening."

That explained the way he looked and the fact that he was wearing the same shirt as yesterday.

"Got something, though," said Norm. "Sandy said the modern rendition of Boland's picture was way off. I've got an appointment for her to talk to Nate's illustrator when she gets back. You might want to hold off on showing the one you have now. Maybe after she gives her input we'll have a more recognizable rendition."

"How about the description–blond hair, brown eyes, 5'11"?"

"Height was right, but she was pretty sure he had blue eyes. He had light brown hair, but Sandy said it might have been dirty blond twenty years ago."

"Your dad is more than happy with what we've got so far. Why don't you go home, take a nap, and clean up? I'll meet you here about 2 pm." Norm didn't need much convincing.

After Norm left, I went to my office and checked off a bunch of items that we would be going over with the team during practice in the days before we left for Europe. They included such things as the different size court, the shorter 3-point line, the ability to touch the ball within the cylinder, and different balls. I'd ordered a dozen European balls, which not only felt different from the Wilson model that was standard for NCAA play but looked different as well. The European ball was two-colored, with a white panel separating the brown ones, and it was larger by 7/10 of an inch.

I started making a list for the coaching staff, starting with the different court and 3-point dimensions. A second sheet listed the differences in game rules. The third listed the differences in coaches' responsibilities, like the fact that only coaches, not players, could call a time out. I ran all three by D'Jarl before I finalized them and gave them to Tip.

The lists done, I went to the cafeteria, hoping to clear my mind with a soft drink and a burrito. It partially worked. I was still a little tired, so I grabbed a cup of coffee to take back as well. That did the trick. I got back to my desk ready to switch gears and think more about Madison Francis and her possible relationship with Lester Fisher.

We'd gone over all the relationships between Lester Fisher and Stemple and our list of suspects. What we hadn't done was look at any relationship between Madison and Fisher. Don't be too hard on yourself, I thought. Neither Nate nor Norm had thought of looking either. Maybe if Mike Ronning were here, he would have caught our mistake, but Mike was probably halfway through his river cruise on his way to Vienna.

After an hour and a half, I'd come up with nothing. As far as I could tell, Fisher and Madison had never met. They didn't even have the same dentist. I had the feeling I was missing something, but unlike other times when I'd had that feeling, I didn't think I would ever discover what it was.

Norm returned at 2:30 looking much better. It looked like he'd washed his hair, or at least showered. He'd changed clothes and the dark rings under his eyes were reduced to smudges. He had in his hands a coffee mug and a quart of orange juice, medium pulp.

"On the mend?" I said, unable to hide my smile.

"It's a good thing I learned the use of meditation for healing while I was in India," replied Norm with the same good humor. "What have you been doing since I left?"

"Trying to find a connection between Fisher and Madison Francis. Came up with zilch. I even checked Fisher's log that Whistel provided and I can't find any mention that Fisher ever went to Stemple's office."

"I forgot to mention that Sandy remembered one other thing about Leroy Boland. He had a gold Rolex, which he wore on his left wrist. She and Madison looked it up after the first date. If it was real, it would cost over 38 thousand dollars. Sandy thinks now that it was probably as phony as he was."

"Left wrist usually means that he's right handed," I said.

"I couldn't find anything about a watch in the police report or the eye witnesses' descriptions of the murderer," said Norm.

I would check in with Stemple the next day and ask him about the watch, and what hand had pulled the trigger when the guy shot Madison. It was a small thing, but it might lead to something.

Rolex watches were not something that I was familiar with, let alone their cost. I had a Timex stopwatch that I used for timing sprint speeds, but I seldom carried it otherwise. I went to my computer and searched for Rolex. I was astounded at the number of models and their costs. There were at least ten gold examples, many with different colored faces.

"Did she mention what color the face was?"

"No."

I turned the computer so Norm could see the different examples. "Ask her when she gets back. I can't imagine many of these are sold at this price. They probably have a registry. We might be able to develop a list of owners."

We kicked around what we had for a while but couldn't think of anything to pursue until Sandy Harper flew back in, which was good. I had enough going on with practice about to start and Michelle still dropping things on me like wedding arbors. It was something that never would have crossed my mind, and now it was all I could picture. Like the different-sized European ball, it was important. I wondered what else I was going to have to worry about.

Still, with the probability of a better photo, the mention of a Rolex worn on the left wrist, and a connection between Madison and Fisher less of a possibility, things were beginning to add up. We just needed some piece of information that would tie the bits we already had together.

CHAPTER 28

I pulled into the school's underground parking lot the next morning and saw that Tip's car was already there. I was looking forward to tomorrow, when the team would begin their official practice for the European trip. D'Jarl had arranged for the court to be striped with the international dimensions. We had a rack of Molten GG7X balls that would be the only ones the team used until we left. I needed to check with the Spanish officials and make sure it would be the model they planned to use for the game ball. It could be handled with a phone call. I'd suggest it to Tip.

The possibility of the two balls made me think of what Norm had said: that the only person who knew what Leroy Boland looked like was Sandy Harper. That wasn't true. There was another. Buddy Doyle knew Buzz. He might not know him as Leroy, but he knew him. Nate might have been premature in dropping him as a client. I wondered if it would be possible to get an illustrator to visit Buddy with me the next morning. If not, there was nothing left to do but await Sandy Harper's return.

Nate had found out that he was still on the police's list as Doyle's attorney. He hadn't received a court order approving his being dropped. Evidently the judge from the arraignment had been reluctant to free Nate of his responsibility to Doyle and was checking for precedents as to conflict of interest. I was at the jail at 10 am. Nate had to get special permission for the illustrator to accompany me with his computer into the room with Buddy Doyle. I asked Nate what he could offer Doyle if he became uncooperative. Nate just grunted.

It was 10:45 when the illustrator, Tony Touloni, and I were escorted back to see Doyle. We went through security and the metal detector. Tony had to leave his computer case and charger and bring only his computer into the interview room. Buddy Doyle was not like Stewart Stemple. Doyle seemed to accept the jail time. The only thing he had in common with Stemple was that he was upset because he wanted to talk to Nate. I told him that Nate was trying to find some way to continue representing him. It was a semi-truth. I didn't feel good about it, but it was what Nate had told me to say. I was surprised I was still on Doyle's visitors' list. I introduced Tony Touloni and showed Doyle the photo of an aged Leroy Boland.

"Do you know this man?"

"Why do you want to know?" asked Doyle. "When will I see Hart again?"

"Please answer my question. I've told you that Mr. Hart is working on trying to get back on your case. Do you know this man?"

"It looks something like Buzz, but not very much."

"Tony has the photo on his computer. Would you help him refine it?"

"No. Why are you so interested in Buzz? I told you he just wanted me to look in the car. He had nothing to do with the robbery except for saying that he didn't want the gun."

"If you want my help and Nate as your attorney, you'll do what I ask," I said. "What are the differences between the way Buzz looks now and this photo?"

For the next fifteen minutes, the two made modifications to the picture, both the front and profile views. The ears were smaller, the nose slightly broken, the cheeks slimmer, and the mouth wider. I could see that it resembled the driver's license photo without the facial grimaces and obvious distortions.

"That's Buzz," said Doyle as the three of us looked at the face on the computer screen.

"Did you ever know him as Leroy Boland?"

For the first time since I'd met him, Buddy Doyle looked worried. Before he'd looked upset with Nate for not showing up, but now his expression was one of fear.

"Why did you call him Leroy? That's Buzz."

"Leroy Boland is the name he goes by now and for the last twenty years."

"Damn. So that's what this is about. You're after Leroy Boland."

"Yes. What can you tell us about him?"

"If I knew who you were after, I wouldn't have told you anything. Going to jail is a lot better than ending up dead."

"The more you can tell us about Boland, the safer you will be," I said.

Tony Touloni folded up his computer. "Can I go now? I can print these up and get them to Nate by the time you're finished here."

"Sure," I said. I got up and pressed the door buzzer.

When Tony had been let out, I turned back to Buddy Doyle, who now was sitting with his hands clasped in front of him, looking defiant.

"Look, I know this much," I said, feeling that Doyle was through talking. "Leroy 'Buzz' Boland is your ticket to getting out of here. I talked with Nate on the way here. You're up for a minimum 15 to 25 years for the robbery and shooting. If you help with Leroy Boland, he could get it down to two or three years, but it will take all your cooperation."

I could see Doyle weighing the possibilities. Finally he said, "How long do you have Buzz going down for?"

"Life."

Again Doyle seemed to be weighing the consequences of talking. "I'm already screwed from what I've given you, even though I didn't know that Buzz was Leroy Boland. Leroy is one of the biggest drug suppliers in the area. No one ever sees him. I didn't even know he was Buzz. He delivers the stuff to a post office box and sends his buyer the key, never in person, and only after he's been paid. I've never heard of him cheating anyone, and anyone who tries to cheat him just disappears. Talk is that he used to deal but took over distribution when his supplier got capped."

"Do you buy from him?"

"Nah. I don't do heavy drugs, and even if I did, I wouldn't be near big enough to deal with Leroy."

"Can you give me the name of someone who would?"

"If I was out, I could probably get you a name or two, but offhand, no. Like I said, I don't deal in drugs."

"Fine. I warn you, no more grand-standing. Also, keep your mouth shut about what you've told me. San Francisco Jail is famous for its snitches, and Leroy might have friends inside." I got up and left. Any chance of going by Nate's and getting the new photos was shot by the time I'd taken with Doyle. I had to get back for the first practice. Just ten more days until we left for Spain. I thought about what Doyle had said about Leroy being big time into the distribution of drugs. If he was that high up, he probably had contacts in the police force.

I phoned Nate on the way to the school. He wasn't in. Linda told me that Tony Touloni was printing out a series of photos on the color printer. I asked her to save four of them for Norm and me and to please email me the image as well.

The players were all on the practice court floor shooting when I entered the Malloy Center. As I walked by, Domingo tossed me a ball. It was one of the European Molten ones. It was obviously different from the Wilsons we were used to. The little knobs on it were more prominent. It also felt a lot bigger than the half-inch on the specs. Only Bogdan was smiling. Balls were clanking off the rim from every player except him. I hoped they would get used to the ball in the next ten days.

"Practice a lot of bounce passes," I shouted at Domingo, as I bounced him the ball. "It will soften the texture like a game ball."

"What do you think?" asked Tip, who was standing next to D'Jarl and Johnny Connor, his second assistant.

"It's definitely different."

"Not the ball. How long do you think it will take for them to get used to it?"

"D'Jarl would be a better judge of that," I said. "Maybe three or four days for the wings–a little longer for the guards," I added, seeing the look of disapproval on Tip's face after my first answer.

"It'll take longer for the players with smaller hands," said D'Jarl, trying to take the heat off me.

"Today we'll have a normal practice," said Tip. "I want them to believe that this is nothing new. The only thing I want you to stress is the new court dimensions. Be hard on anyone who steps out of bounds. I don't think the shorter three-point line will be a factor. It might be if it was longer, but we're used to shooting from further out, and that will spread the defenses we face."

"What did you tell Domingo?" asked Tip.

"I told him to practice a lot of bounce passes. Try to wear down some of the texture. It didn't seem to bounce back quite as quickly as our ball. We should check the air pressure."

"That's been done," said D'Jarl. "All are to spec."

"Johnny, you might get a dozen cones and set up a dribbling course. Four feet between cones."

We continued to watch in silence. The majority of the team had been together for two years. They knew how Tip ran his practices. They were showing the new guys, Booker Oowaite and D'Andre Blaston, what to expect. I hoped they wouldn't be worn out by the time practice started.

Half an hour later, the players were warmed up. Tip concentrated on shooting and dribbling, interspersed with a few wind sprints, but not as many as he would have done normally. Two hours later, with the last twenty minutes spent on free throws, we were finished. Tip was happy.

"Good first day," said Tip. "Everybody seems in shape. I suspect they'll be sore tomorrow, though. More of the same for two more days, then we'll start working on plays and schemes. You all are to go over the game films for the teams we will play and give me your thoughts on the Spanish team tomorrow at ten in the film room." Tip turned to his office and closed the door.

It was 3:15. Norm wasn't in his office. I had the game films on my computer. I'd watch them at home. Sandy Harper was coming in late morning the following day and Norm was picking her up. It was no longer so vital that she go over the photo with the illustrator after what we had gotten from Buddy Doyle, but I suspected she could still add some details. Details were important.

CHAPTER 29

I made a phone call to Nate on the way to school, confirming that Buddy Doyle had verified that Buzz and Leroy Boland were one and the same. I recounted that Doyle had been cooperative, but that he was afraid for his life when he found out that Buzz was Leroy Boland.

The coaches' meeting was in the film room, with each of the staff going over what they had seen in the tapes of the Spanish national squad. The consensus was that it was going to be a hard game to win. They were big, fast, and talented, especially in the guard position. D'Jarl and I shared our thoughts on how to play them. Johnny Connor was silent for the most part, as he was still getting used to his role as second assistant. We could hear the sounds of balls bouncing and shoes squeaking in the background as the players warmed up like they had the previous day.

"Practice starts in half an hour," said Tip. "Tomorrow, same time, and we'll go over our plan for the French team."

"I went to dinner last night," said D'Jarl to Tip as the others filed out. "I stopped by here to pick up my computer with the game films. The lights were on in Malloy. The whole team was in there shooting except for Oowaite and Blaston, who had a night class. They might be a little slow today."

D'Jarl's prediction was false. The kids were just as feisty, just as fresh as they had been the day before. The four amigos–Jackson, Damari, Domingo, and Danny Priest–had spent the summer in Sacramento working out together, just as they had the year before. That summer Avery Pierson had spent a couple weeks at Jackson's house, working out under the eye of Damari's father. They had started the fall semester in great shape and maintained it all season. Today's practice was just like the day before. The buzzer went off at 3 pm, and the coaches left the gym. The players didn't. Youth is a wonderful thing.

I changed my shoes, grabbed my backpack with my laptop in it, and went down the stairs to Norm's office. He wasn't there. I was leaving through the main lobby doors when I met Norm coming in with Sandy Harper, who was still dressed in her flight attendant's uniform. She had been up all night working a non-stop flight from Frankfurt but still looked better than Norm. He was dressed in the same clothes he'd had on yesterday after his nap. His slacks were rumpled, his shirt clean but limp looking. Eve, I thought. Well, better her than Sandy Harper; I remembered Nate's warning.

"I picked up Sandy at the airport," said Norm. "She was hungry so we went to lunch. I'm about to take her to Nate's office to see if we can get the illustrator to give us a better likeness."

"Yesterday after you left, I remembered that the fellow who damaged your car might also know Leroy. I took the illustrator to him and he helped refine the image."

I took my laptop out of my backpack and pulled up my emails. I was hoping that Nate's assistant, Linda, had sent the new image. There it was, fourth down in my unanswered list. I clicked on it, and the color photo of Leroy Boland filled the screen. I swung the computer so that Sandy could see it.

"That's him. His eyebrows grow a little closer together and his hair is parted differently, but it's him."

Norm moved to Sandy's side and looked at the screen. His eyes, which had just before been slits, opened wide. "I know this guy!" he exclaimed.

"Sandy!" I yelled her name to get her attention and to stop Norm from saying anything else. "There's a chance that Leroy Boland murdered Madison. That means that you are in danger."

"Why?" asked Sandy, obviously not believing me, or at least not understanding why she would be.

"We've learned more about this guy since we last talked. Now that you've identified him, it's important that you don't go back to your apartment and that you don't use your phone. You're the only solid link between Leroy and Madison. It's important that you stay safe until he's behind bars."

Norm looked confused, not understanding why I didn't want Sandy to know Boland's other name.

"Norm, would you take Sandy to the Hilton on Union Square and check her in?"

"I need to stop by my place and get some clothes," said Sandy.

"That's exactly what you shouldn't do," I said, firmly. "Norm can take you shopping after you check in at the Hilton. Get anything you need for the next few days. It's on us."

"I'm not supposed to fly for two days, but I am on call. I need to answer if they call."

"You can't. Boland might be able to trace your location by your phone. Keep it off, or better yet, let Norm hold it for you." I motioned for her phone and turned it completely off, then handed it to Norm. "Norm, could I speak to you for a minute? We'll be right back."

We went to the lobby of the gym, where we were alone. "Who is this guy?" I asked.

"Remember we originally had eleven on the list of people wanting to get even with Fisher? Then we trimmed it to four after checking alibis. I put one guy back on, even though he had a solid alibi, just because he was in the building at the time of the shooting. That's the guy, Lance LaBarr. I interviewed him the day my car was broken into."

"The guy in the cafeteria with a woman as his alibi," I said. "We both checked her out. His alibi is solid."

"Who cares? I'm sure. Leroy 'Buzz' Boland and Lance LaBarr are the same guy," said Norm.

"Either that or twins. I think you should stay with Sandy. Nate will surely want to hide her from the police and the DA until we can nail down LaBarr. Get her checked into the hotel. Take her shopping. Take her to dinner. But don't tell her LaBarr's name. We don't know if he has contacts in the police department, and if Inspector Farley gets hold of her, she will tell him. You interviewed LaBarr, so you might be in danger as well. Be careful. I'll tell Nate what we've found out so far and call you if we need anything more from Sandy. He might want her to refine Doyle's photo rendition."

We went back to Norm's office. I purposely flashed my badge as we sat down. "Sandy, this is extremely serious. We're lucky that you've been out of town and that Norm picked you up. It will only take a couple of days to arrest Leroy. When we do, you'll be safe, but until then, do exactly what Norm says."

She nodded, first to me, then to Norm. "How do you know Leroy?" she asked Norm.

"He was someone we saw in a surveillance video. Now that you've identified him, he's toast." Norm told the lie perfectly, and Sandy seemed satisfied.

I took them to the underground garage and drove them to where Norm had parked, then drove to Nate's office, phoning him on the way.

—

I waited half an hour for Nate, using the time to go over the interview I'd had with Julie Wessenberg. I was almost sure that she was telling the truth about meeting LaBarr for the first time that morning. As I read her answers, I realized that she hadn't mentioned the two fire alarms that had sounded–just one. I was about to listen to the telephone recording that George Krusen had sold to Nate when he burst into the office.

"Tell me you have something good," Nate said as he closed the door and took his seat.

"I think we have the murderer. It turns out Leroy Boland is the same person as Lance LaBarr. LaBarr was in the building when the murders took place. He'd been sued by Fisher and had fought with Madison Francis, who had seen evidence of his dual identity. He's also the guy who ordered the break-in of Norm's car."

"What about an alibi?"

"Both Norm and I interviewed a woman who LaBarr said was having breakfast with him in the building's cafeteria at the time of the shootings. It seemed solid, but now I think I can break it using the recordings Krusen and Whistel have provided."

"Use Krusen's recording. It wouldn't be hard to identify Whistel, and that would get him fired," said Nate. "If it comes to it, I can subpoena him as a hostile witness and get it that way."

After purchasing Krusen's recording, Nate remembered that Whistel was also on the phone and he'd obtained a copy of that recording as well. The clarity was not as good as Krusen's, but it was more dramatic, with the screams, the gunshots, and the yelling of the murderer as he left.

"I'm trying to find a connection between LaBarr and Stemple. That would give him a motive for all three—the murders of Fisher and Madison, and the framing of Stemple."

Nate opened his desk drawer and took out a file. He removed a copy of the list of the names of people Stemple had screwed. "No LaBarr," said Nate, shooting the page across his desk. He was correct–no mention of Lance LaBarr, but third from the bottom was Leroy Boland.

"Bingo," I said, showing Nate the name. "What more do we need to give this guy to the police?"

"Break his alibi," said Nate. "Find out the details of what Stemple did to him. Do a complete background check on his finances, familiarity with firearms, and where his office is located in 560 Mission. Norm can help you with that."

"I've got Norm babysitting Madison Francis's roommate. I told her she was in danger, which she might be, but I mainly thought you would want to hide her from the police until we nailed LaBarr."

Nate looked up, a smile on his face. "Have you ever thought about law school? That was good thinking. Where is she?"

"I told Norm to check her into the Hilton and buy her clothes for a couple of days. I said to stick with her. I'm sure Inspector Farley would like to talk to her and I didn't want her going back to her apartment. Also, early on, Norm interviewed LaBarr. He might be in danger as well."

"The Hilton? Better clear this up fast or my expense sheet is going to get out whack."

I didn't bother telling Nate that my remaining days as his investigator were coming to an end soon as well. I left the office. There was still time to get to the jail and talk with Stewart Stemple. On the way over, I called Michelle.

"Honey," I said after she picked up. "You know how you asked if you could help with my case? I have a big ask. Could you do a complete financial check on Lance LaBarr and Stewart Stemple? Also, see if there's anything on Leroy Boland as far as dealing with either of the others."

"Sure," said Michelle. "I thought you had Norm helping you?"

"He wouldn't be nearly as thorough as you, and besides, he's on another assignment."

"When do you need this?"

"Yesterday. LaBarr and Boland are the same person. Different identities."

"Wow. I'll get on it right now."

We said goodbye, Michelle saying she might have something by dinner.

Julie Wessenberg, LaBarr's alibi, was my next call. I only had the bakery's number. She wasn't there. They wouldn't give me her cell, so I told them to phone her, give her my name, and tell her it was urgent–a matter of great importance.

"Julie is probably asleep. She'll be in to bake at five tomorrow morning," said the woman at the bakery.

I hoped that she would return my call tonight. If not, tomorrow at five am would have to do.

CHAPTER 30

It seemed like ages since Michelle and I had had pizza for dinner. I called Red Boy, and they had the pizza ready for pickup by the time I got there.

I had to wait a few minutes for a backhoe to clear the street in front of a house that was being worked on just down the block from mine. We'd traded a garage for a bedroom. This place was adding a full upper floor. Dirt and debris were all over the sidewalk and half the street.

I'd been running pretty much all day. That made a shower a necessity. I sat under the hot water for a long time, relaxing, feeling the tension I was under wash away with the flow of water over my head and shoulders. I'd just dried off and changed into my sweats when Michelle came in with a pizza from Red Boy. When she saw the pizza box on the counter, we both laughed. Great minds think alike. We threw mine in the refrigerator. I set the table and made a salad while Michelle did a quick change of clothes.

I dominated the conversation while we ate the pizza, which was sharply divided in half–anchovies on my side, none of the little fishes on hers. I told her how we had learned that Leroy Boland and Lance LaBarr were the same person, how Norm had made the connection after he'd seen the altered photo. As we finished our last slices, I told her I was going to get up early the next morning to talk to the baker, Julie Wessenberg, for a second time.

Michelle just smiled and said nothing until we had both finished. "We ate my pie. You clean up." She got up and went into the front room. When I finished, I joined her. She was sitting on the couch with a stack of printouts on the coffee table in front of her.

"These will interest you," she said. "These show the activity on all the accounts for Boland-LaBarr and your Mr. Stemple. We knew that Boland had a savings account at a bank in San Rafael. It turns out he has an overseas account, in fact several of them, with a lot more in them than he keeps here. James is sure he'll be able to get more information tomorrow."

"James?" I asked.

"James Armbruster. You've met him a couple times. He's a computer genius. He'll have more by tomorrow."

"Sure, Armbruster. Tall, thin guy. You sent him out for wine, size 14 feet. He got all this since I phoned you?"

"Yes. He's used to getting into the accounts of the people who request gifts from the foundation. You'd be surprised at how many are fraudulent or trying to hide their true worth."

"Can you give me the Reader's Digest version?"

"Basically, about one in four of the transactions is a large sum, run from and to the offshore accounts. Boland-LaBarr is obviously a crook, but your guy Stemple is just as bad."

"If this goes to court, James will have to spend time explaining this to Nate's forensic accountant. It could add up to earning James a trip to Disneyland."

I figured that Julie Wessenberg's early start was to do the baking of the croissants or at least supervise it. I didn't see what getting there at five would do for me that six-thirty wouldn't. When the alarm went off at 5:15, I wasn't ready to roll.

Michelle had set up the coffee the night before, and its aroma was what finally got me out of bed. I dressed quickly, poured the coffee into a thermos, and went to my car. It was listing strangely to the driver's side in the driveway. The driver's side front tire was flat to the rim. I remembered the construction going on down the street and swore under my breath. I was about to open the trunk and get out the spare when I remembered I was a two-car guy now. I went back into the house, grabbed the keys to the Viper and the opener to Mrs. O'Reilly's garage, and shot out the door, almost forgetting my thermos of coffee.

I found a parking spot on the street in front of the bakery, secured a club to my steering wheel (something I never had to do with my Camry), and went inside. With nobody manning the front, I opened the door to the back. As I thought, Julie was tending the ovens.

"Miss Wessenberg," I yelled over the noise.

Julie looked over at me and said a few words to one of her helpers, who was dressed in a white apron and cap.

"You're not allowed back here," she said, making a shooing motion at me with her hands as we moved into the front area. It was almost 6:30. "I got your message this morning but I didn't want to call you before eight."

"I'd just like to ask you a few questions and have you to listen to a recording that was made the morning of the shooting. It's very important."

"How long is the recording?" asked Julie.

"About fifteen minutes. It was taken while you were in the cafeteria." She looked at her cell phone.

"All right, but I'll have to go back inside in eight minutes. Is it something we can split up?"

"Sure." I brought up Franklin Whistel's recording on my phone and turned up the volume. Krusen's didn't have good sound of the shots. They came over as indistinct pops. There was no naming of Whistel on the recording Wessenberg was hearing. I hoped Nate wouldn't be too mad. "There's a conversation that isn't important. What I want you to listen to is the background noise, gunshots, alarms, and PA announcements." I pressed play.

The timing of the ovens couldn't have been more inconvenient. The first fire alarm had just sounded when her phone alarm went off; Wessenberg got up and left. She was back in less than five minutes, holding a plate with two croissants, one of which she offered to me with a warning to let it cool for a minute.

"I've turned the recording back," I said. Once again we heard the gunshots, then a man shouting a warning not to try to leave or call the police or he'd come back. Then, after less than a minute, we heard the faint sounds of three more gunshots over the screams of the people in Fisher's office. The alarm went on for about three minutes, then stopped. We could barely hear the conversation between Whistel and his client over the din. There were another three minutes of screams, then Whistel's client asking if those were gunshots and Whistel saying that they were and he was all right. Then the fire alarm sounded again. Three minutes later, there was an announcement over the building's PA that there had been a shooting and everyone should remain where they were until the police had cleared the building.

"You said that you heard the fire alarm and the announcement about the police. Did you hear the first fire alarm or just the second?" Julie Wessenberg's answer was critical to LaBarr's alibi.

"No, I only heard one, then the shooting announcement and the police sirens. You can barely hear them on the recording."

"The recording was made on the 32nd floor," I explained. "Can you estimate when in the recording Lance LaBarr came over to your table?"

"It was after the shooting announcement was made. Thirty seconds to a minute later. He was a calming influence. People were starting to panic. A man was screaming that he had to leave."

"Thank you very much for making time for me this morning," I said, "and for the croissant." There it was: an almost perfect timeline from the shooting and Leroy "Buzz" Boland sharing the table with Julie Wessenberg. His alibi, which had sounded perfect initially, was not so perfect after all.

I went to my car. It was four minutes until 7. I considered the pluses and minuses of an early phone call, then dialed Inspector Farley. He answered quickly and didn't sound upset.

"You ready to tell me about Buzz?" he asked, having seen who was calling.

"I'm ready to tell you a lot more than that," I said. "I'm going to give you the man who committed the murders at 560."

"I don't play lawyers' games," said Farley.

"I know you believe you have your man," I said, trying to sound as reasonable as I could. "Even though the hair that was planted in the mask should give you pause. Please just listen. Mr. Hart doesn't know I'm calling you."

"All right," said Farley, sounding slightly appeased but still skeptical.

"Buzz's full name is Leroy 'Buzz' Boland." I thought it best to hit Farley with the big reveal, since he might have a file on him. "We've got a witness who will confirm that he's a major drug dealer. You know from Madison Francis's datebook that they had a fight. What you might not know is that it was because she'd discovered that Buzz Boland had another identity–Lance LaBarr. Sandy Harper, Madison's roommate, will confirm that. LaBarr has an office in 560 Mission and was in the building when the murders were committed. His alibi starts nine minutes after the first shots."

"Sounds to me like your boss has a good alternative, but not necessarily the murderer," said Farley, not sounding so pleased anymore.

"There's more. Besides Madison discovering LaBarr's dual identity, Fisher had just sued LaBarr for a large sum. And Stemple had a business deal go sour for LaBarr as well. So, you now have motives for killing Fisher and Francis and for framing Stemple, plus opportunity and ability. Oh, I didn't mention that he fits the general description of the shooter."

"You can prove all this?"

"Yes. I know that Leroy Boland had a serious falling out with Stewart Stemple. I'd like to know exactly what it was, but I won't be able to see Stemple until after 10 am. I think that if Boland-LaBarr had one false identity, he probably has another, or several others. He's a definite flight risk. You should put him behind bars before he cuts out."

"I could get you in to see Stemple at 8 am," said Farley. "We could talk to him together."

"Fantastic. I'll meet you at the jail, but we might need to wait if either Stemple or Doyle insists that Hart be present."

As soon as Farley hung up, I phoned Nate. Unlike Farley, he was not happy to be called this early in the morning. It took fifteen minutes for me to relate everything I'd told Farley and to answer Nate's other questions.

"The DA and the police will be interested in nailing LaBarr for the murder," said Nate, "if only because they know they'll never be able to win the case against Stemple with such an obvious alternative suspect. The problem is that I'm in Sacramento and tied up here most the day."

"I really think we're liable to lose LaBarr if he even senses that anything's closing in on him. He might even have a connection in the police department. It's why I jumped the gun in telling Inspector Farley, so we could get to Stemple immediately."

"Bring Norm with you. He's a lawyer. I'll call him right now and tell him what to do."

"Perfect. I'm only a few blocks from the Hilton. We can go together."

"Hilton? Isn't that where you're stashing the girl?"

"Yes. Norm says he knows what you said about an involvement. He said that the room had two beds and that he'd behave."

"Give me fifteen minutes with him," said Nate and hung up.

I sat in my car and waited to call Norm. In the time that I sat there with the top down, three men and one woman stopped on the sidewalk to admire the Viper. One of the men said, "I didn't think they made those anymore." He was astounded when I told him it was a 2002, over twenty-three years old. It looked brand new.

I waited an extra four minutes before I phoned Norm. It was 7:42. The jail was just an eight-minute drive from the Hilton. I figured that Norm would be dressed and ready to go after talking to his dad. I was right. He was waiting for me on the curb three minutes later. His clothes were new–no sign of the Eve attire from yesterday. I suspected he'd stopped at his apartment on his way to taking Sandy Harper to the Hilton.

I called Inspector Farley and asked if he would let us park in the police lot. I was worried about leaving the Viper on the street. Farley was waiting at the lift gate. He looked curiously at the Viper as he opened the gate and Norm and I pulled in and parked. It was five minutes before eight. The three of us entered the building together.

"Stemple should be in the interview room by now," said Farley as we approached the counter.

"Before we see Stemple, we must talk with Buddy Doyle," said Norm.

"Buddy Doyle?" asked Farley. "What does he have to do with this?"

"Everything. He's the key to understanding the 560 murders," said Norm. "After we speak with him, we can see Mr. Stemple."

Nate had obviously given Norm instructions that I knew nothing about. I nodded when Farley looked at me for confirmation.

"Mr. Doyle can link Leroy Boland to Lance LaBarr," said Norm to Farley. "He can prove that Leroy, whom he knows as Buzz, hired him to rob my car, taking a file on the case, some insurance documents, and my registered handgun. The police weren't interested in the break-in, only in whether my weapon was unsecured." Norm was unable to stop himself from being snide. I suspected he was still burning about the DA wanting to charge him for leaving an unsecured firearm. "He can also provide you with information about Boland being a major drug dealer. There's more as well, that is, if we can come to an agreement on his charges."

"I would have to discuss that with the District Attorney," said Farley.

"I believe my father is already doing that," said Norm. "Attempted murder and robbery with a gun carry a sentence of 20 years. We would fight that, of course, and get it lowered. We have a copy of the robbery surveillance film, and it clearly shows the clerk lowering his hand beneath the counter. Our client fired out of fear that he was going to be shot. Furthermore, he's never used a gun before–never had one until he took mine when he broke into my car. He hadn't even fired the gun in question, which we can prove by checking the fingerprints on the bullets in the magazine. I think they will be mine from over two years ago."

"What are you asking for?"

"Our client knows he's done wrong. Mr. Wong is out of critical care and is recovering, but our client understands that he must answer for what he did. We're asking that his charge be modified to aggravated assault, with a recommended sentence of two years. If his testimony isn't what I've promised, then we'll go to court, but we will have missed a chance to apprehend the real murderer."

"As I said, I'll have to discuss this with the D.A."

"I suggest you do that now," said Norm. "Then call Nate. He will have a message for me."

Farley got up and left the room.

It took only ten minutes for Doyle to be led into the interview room. Farley was gone, still talking with the D.A.

"What's this about?" asked Doyle, looking at me first, then at Norm.

"I'm Norm Hart. Nate is my dad. He's in Sacramento, and he'll see you tomorrow. In the meantime, please consider me your attorney."

"What's this about?" Doyle asked again.

"Hold on until we hear from Inspector Farley. Don't say a word until I say it's okay. Then answer truthfully. But stop immediately if I tell you to. I believe that if you do this, we've negotiated a sweet deal for you."

"Will I still have to do time?"

"You shot a man in an attempted robbery. Of course you'll do time," said Norm. "But we might just have gotten your sentence reduced from twenty years to two, with the possibility of less, if we get the right judge and this plays out the way we hope."

Nothing else was said until Farley reentered the room. It was Norm's show. "All right, you've got your deal," said Farley.

"Did you talk with my father?"

"Yes. He said to tell you, 'Proceed, son. We've got our deal.'"

Proceed, son, was the correct code, signifying that the D.A. had signed off on the reduced sentence.

Norm walked Buddy Doyle through the timeline, starting from when Doyle had gotten the call from Buzz to follow Norm. When Norm returned to 560, Doyle had taken the opportunity to bust into the car and take the gun and the documents. He supplied all the information that we promised, including an identification of the photo of the man he knew as Buzz and the fact that he was a major drug dealer. Norm was satisfied, and so was Farley.

We switched rooms. Stewart Stemple was not happy. He'd been waiting, cuffed to the table, for 45 minutes.

"Before we start," said Norm, showing that he was still leading the meeting, "I want you to know that in giving testimony that will reveal the real murderer, Mr. Stemple might have to implicate himself in some nonviolent illegal acts. He agrees to give this information, as it will directly help in the conviction of the true murderer, instead of taking the 5th Amendment. He will be given immunity from that testimony as a consideration. That too has been agreed upon by the D.A."

I guess I knew more about Boland-LaBarr's guilt than Norm did, because Norm now pushed back his chair and motioned to me. He said, "You're on."

CHAPTER 31

I started with the obvious, showing Stemple both of the pictures and having him identify them as LaBarr. "I don't know Boland," he said. This surprised me, but I tried to keep from showing it.

"But you did business with both of them," I said, trying to recover. The room was exactly the same size as the one we'd seen Buddy Doyle in minutes before, but it suddenly seemed cramped and hot.

"LaBarr referred the other guy, Boland, to me," said Stemple. "He said he was an American citizen living abroad. I never met him."

"What kind of business?"

"At first it was small stuff. Basically establishing an account with my firm. Two years ago he had built up a sizable balance and he wanted me to invest in single-family housing in the Bay Area, primarily in San Francisco and Marin County."

"But your relationship soured. You told me that he became upset with you. Can you explain?"

Stemple seemed reluctant to answer.

"It's all right," I said. "We have an agreement that covers anything you tell us about your dealings with either LaBarr or Boland that was illegal."

"I have immunity?"

"For anything you tell us that helps convict Leroy Boland," I said.

Inspector Farley straightened in his chair. His movement distracted Stemple for a moment. I had to gesture to him to continue. "The first year, I invested less than a million for him. It seemed on the up and up. But, when we started buying houses, he was depositing a couple million dollars every six months. Most of it came through LaBarr, a large part of it in cash. Other large amounts came from various overseas accounts. By the third year, I was handling almost five million a year for him. I realized that he was laundering money. Real estate is one of the few areas in which you can buy with cash without ringing a lot of bells. Three months ago, I bought a property for him. I inflated the sales price and pocketed $300,000 that wasn't on the books, on top of my fees, but Boland found about it. LaBarr told me that he was furious. I figured Boland was a crook and out of the country. What could he do about it? He couldn't go to the police without disclosing the source of the money, and I wanted out anyway."

"Did Madison Francis ever meet Lance LaBarr?"

"Not to my knowledge," said Stemple. "I always went to his office. LaBarr said it was quieter. It was a small office on the 8th floor. He never came to mine."

"Describe LaBarr. We know what he looks like. What size is he?"

"He's my size. Maybe an inch taller."

"We think," I said, realizing what the Fisher-Boland connection probably was, "we will find that Fisher discovered Boland-LaBarr's real estate dealings and was blackmailing him. So," I added, turning to Inspector Farley, "Leroy Boland had dated Madison Francis, using the name Buzz Boland. He had a serious fight with her when she saw his second wallet and discovered he had a dual identity. There's your motive for him killing Madison. Stemple, our client, had stolen from him. But Boland couldn't kill him, as it would expose his operation and cast suspicion on himself and the origins of the money. So he framed Mr. Stemple. If you need more, Mr. Stemple's barber will identify Buddy Doyle as the one who robbed him, took the hair that you found in the mask, and gave it to Buzz."

Norm looked at me and pursed his lips. This was something we didn't know for sure. We had forgotten to ask Doyle about it in the other room.

"I told you the gunman seemed to hesitate when he saw Madison by my side," said Stemple. "It was like he was surprised to see her. He moved the gun from me and shot her twice."

It was enough. There was more, but we'd given Farley enough to detain LaBarr.

"I'll remind you that the murderer probably has more than one false identity," I said to Farley. "He's a real risk to run."

Farley got up and pushed the button to be released from the room. Norm and I followed.

"I'll phone security at 560 and find out if he's in the building," said the inspector as we moved quickly towards the front of the station. "If he's there, I'll have them secure the building. We'll put him under arrest now."

"Would you mind if we tagged along?" I asked. "Norm and I have been working hard on getting this evidence and would like to see it through."

Inspector Farley hesitated, then said, "Follow us. We'll park in 560's garage. Promise to keep out of the way. We almost lost you last year. I don't want any more accusations about using you as bait."

"Promise," I said.

Norm looked at me questioningly. I would tell him about it on the way to 560.

———

It was a small procession–two police cars, no sirens, no flashing lights, and one yellow Dodge Viper with its top down–that drove the few blocks from the jail to 560 Mission Street. Inspector Farley pulled up to the entrance to the garage and spoke to the guard, who raised the gate and waved us through. I was level with the attendant when there was a squeal of tires and a black M 8 BMW coupe pulled up across from me, leaving the garage.

"That's him!" shouted Norm, pointing across me at the driver of the BMW. Just then an alarm sounded and the roll-down security gate started coming down. The BMW lurched out of the garage, just under the closing gate, and turned west.

I threw my car into reverse and shot back out onto the street. The metal gate slammed down on the pavement, just missing my front bumper. The police cars were locked inside. I turned down the street to see the BMW already half a block ahead of me. I threw Viper into first and stomped on the throttle. The car fishtailed as the tires caught purchase on the asphalt and shot forward, with me barely able to hold it in a straight line.

Damn, I thought, as I steered the Viper around traffic, using the Bus Only lane. Only Norm, Farley, and I had known we were coming for LaBarr. Then the obvious answer came to me: Julie Wessenberg. She still thought LaBarr was a nice man.

The BMW was speeding, weaving in and out of traffic, and then it took a left turn on 3rd Street. I followed, noticing that I had made up distance and was now only two cars behind the black sedan. I grabbed my phone from my pocket and passed it to Norm, who was holding on for dear life.

"Call Farley," I screamed over the rush of wind. "It should be the last number dialed. Tell him where we are and that we have LaBarr in sight."

The BMW moved to the right lane and ran a red light, heading for the freeway onramp to 101. A car passed in front of me, causing me to brake, but then a small opening allowed me to floor it and we went through the red light as well. Horns blew. I ignored them. We'd only lost a little on the BMW. There were now four cars between us.

I heard Norm giving our location to the police. The BMW again moved to the right and took the turnoff to 101 West, headed for Hayes Valley. If the car got to Hayes Valley, with its parks and convoluted streets, there was a good chance we'd lose it, no matter how fast my car was. Traffic was only moderately heavy, but almost as soon as we were on the elevated freeway, the traffic in front of us started to slow and compress. I knew the freeway well. It was my go-to route from USF to the South Bay when I used 101. There was no way off it until it emptied at its end onto Octavia Boulevard. The BMW was just two cars ahead of me when it came to a stop, with no place to go. A police car had done slowing S curves in front of us and stopped all traffic on the freeway.

I started to get out, then remembered Farley warning me to stay safe. He was right. I'd rather attend my wedding than my funeral. LaBarr had already killed two people. Another wouldn't matter much. A siren from behind caused me to slam my door. A San Francisco motorcycle cop sped past me, threading his way between cars. Coming from the front, two highway patrolmen on foot made their way through the stopped cars. I watched as LaBarr opened his door, got out, and ran to the side of the freeway. It was on stilts, and on the side thirty feet away were offices and a Costco outlet. LaBarr looked over. It was at least a four-story drop to the pavement. He paused as if about to leap, then stopped, dropped a handgun over the railing, and put his hands above his head. More sirens came from behind, and more police rushed by on foot, guns drawn. It was over.

Norm passed me the phone. "Farley wants to talk with you."

"Yes, Inspector?"

"I thought I told you to stay safe," he said. He sounded official and mad. "Thanks for not listening. We wouldn't have caught him if you hadn't followed him and given us directions. Meet me at the jail. It will be good to finish this off. I'll leave word at the parking lot. I'll even station an officer to watch your car."

I was going to miss practice. I hoped Tip would understand and would be happy that the drop-dead date I'd given him for working with Nate would expire five days early. He would join Michelle as president of that club.

EPILOGUE

The morning of the second day after Lance LaBarr's arrest, Stewart Stemple was released on bail. The District Attorney kept the charge for the murder of Madison Francis on him, just in case the indictment for Lance LaBarr fell apart. She was concerned that the evidence we'd uncovered implicating LaBarr was mostly circumstantial. She was sure she could get him on drug trafficking and money laundering, but there was no direct evidence connecting him to any of the murders. That is, until Nate turned over Franklin Whistel's recording of the events that had taken place in Fisher's office. Her expert quickly confirmed, with 98% accuracy, that the voice of the man who'd shouted as he left the office after killing Fisher and wounding Kirsten Grant was LaBarr's. The police had also found LaBarr's duplicate wallet identifying him as Leroy "Buzz" Boland in the glove compartment of his BMW.

The DA was concerned that there was no contact DNA linking Boland-LaBarr to the killings. He'd worn gloves, and the hat dropped in Stemple's lobby was a plant. They did recover the knife that Buddy Doyle had used in the robbery of the hair salon, and it still had traces of Forsythe's blood on the blade. This made Buddy's testimony even more damning.

Mike Ronning had returned early, forgoing his London stop. It took me the better part of an evening to go over the case with him. He laughed when I told him it was the break-in of Norm's car–something the police had ignored–and the subsequent use of the stolen handgun in a robbery of a mom-and-pop convenience store that had led to Buddy Doyle and eventually Leroy Boland. He agreed with me that the DA had probably influenced the discovery reporting of the hair in the mask to bolster her own case. When I related the chase of LaBarr in the Viper, Ronning laughed out loud and called me Steve McQueen.

Norm started dating Sandy Harper. He also had a couple dinner dates with Barret Sorrenson, who had found her own apartment in North Beach. I suspected he was still seeing Eve Hoversal as well. It had been a week, and every time I saw him, he looked beat. As much as Nate wanted him to stay, I suspected that Norm would have to leave San Francisco, for health reasons if nothing else.

Nate paid me for my time, with a little extra for what Michelle had done. James Armbruster got his trip to Disneyland as well. Michelle and I finally had enough money to make the addition of a bathroom connected to our new bedroom a real possibility. I could also get rid of the Camry, but I didn't need to with the Viper safely garaged two houses down.

I had finished my entire to-do list for the wedding. It was impressed upon me that Michelle's concerns with seating arrangements, flowers, linens, and musicians were as important and as time-consuming as my involvement with Nate's case had been. With the wedding just two weeks away, I was glad that the European trip with the team was coming up in two days. I was already packed.

ACKNOWLEDGEMENTS

Every novel starts somewhere, even before the first word is put on the page. Often it begins with an inspiration. In the case of *MURDER DOUBLE DIPPED*, the inspiration started with my daughter, Adrienne who lived through the security measures I've written about at 560 Mission Street.

A book might only take a few months to write the first draft. Then the real work begins. It is this that I give my thanks to the Mill Valley Library's Author Group.

Kate Moore, a wonderful author of period romance novels. Kate keeps me straight on keeping my women strong, my prose polished, and the plots intriguing.

John Byrne Barry an author of mystery thrillers and plays. John's novels are concerned with social issues that are woven seamlessly with his stories of murder and deceit. John helps me to keep my character's inner thoughts known, making them relevant and more human.

Rob Fisher writes fantasy and poetry. He writes so beautifully that sometimes it's hard to separate the two. He gives me advice as to character motivation.

Matthew Gordon Nelson, a member of SAG, has done the narration of all my books on Audible. I couldn't ask for a better voice for my characters. His reviews support my rather biased opinion of his work. His associate, Scott Brown, as sound editor makes sure the quality of the recording is the best possible.

Adrienne Brown, reads all my work and keeps me on the straight and narrow with all things lawyerly. She is a true professional and a wealth of information.

Brian Van Camerik is responsible for all my covers. I'm amazed that he insists on reading the novel before putting his pen to page, knowing that the best covers help describe the words inside.

My agent Gayle Gladstone at Waterside Publications, and Josh Freel who edits my novels, receive my heartfelt thanks for their talent and expertise.

Last as always, but first in my heart is my wife, Kellie, who puts up with my tippy tapping far into the night.

www.ingramcontent.com/pod-product-compliance
Lightning Source LLC
Chambersburg PA
CBHW071151260626
47162CB00003B/1002